凱信企管

**用對的方法充實自己，
讓人生變得更美好！**

凱信企管

用對的方法充實自己，
讓人生變得更美好！

回溯式學習英語會話

先聽說再讀寫，大量測驗的刻意練習，
提升英語各項能力

序

　　英文是國際間最廣泛用來溝通的語言之一，無論是出國旅遊、留學充電，還是和其他國家的公司有工作上的往來，我們時常會需要借助英文來交流溝通。因此，英文無疑是身處「地球村」的我們應該要掌握的語言工具。英文既然如此重要，但為什麼在我們經歷了國中、高中甚至大學近十年的英語教育之後，英文程度卻是連最簡單的溝通都有問題，或是不敢開口說？難道我們十年的英文都白學了嗎？

　　許多英文學習者都會遇到一個問題，就是「不知道該從哪裡得到日常英文的知識」，它與教科書上艱深、專業、卻不一定有機會使用的英文非常不同。我們無時無刻不在使用，卻同時又難以系統化地整理出來讓人學習。

　　因此，本書的特色就是透過各式各樣的閱讀和聽力測驗，將生活中可能會用到的單字、句型，轉化成故事和習題，並按主題歸類。例如：在「家庭中」，可以知道如何自我介紹、描述他人的髮型與服裝打扮；在「家」中，可以學會閱讀電器的使用說明；在「日常事務」中，可以了解如何流暢記錄自己一整天的日常活動；「出遊」中則是包含了問路、描述地標等，舉凡到不熟悉的地方時，必定會用到的內容。

本書不僅有貼近生活的題材，也有多元又充足的習題，每個unit中都有七個或八個part，而每個part中又設計了多個題組，從判斷文意的是非題、選擇題，到剖析文章重點的問答題，再到自我挑戰、活用所學的寫作，循序漸進地帶領讀者學習。除此之外，本書還整理了許多表述時的正式和非正式用語、英式英文和美式英文的差別、同一個單字的正面和負面意義的使用等，能讓學習者更精確地區別語言的細微之處，培養語感。同時，對於想透過本書練習口語的學習者，本書特別收錄了每個單元的錄音文木，讓學習者能聽錄音校正自己的發音和語調，並模擬對話，自我練習，聽力口語同步訓練、提升。

　　最後要提醒各位學習者，處處留心皆學問，只要好好觀察自己周邊的生活，必定能找到許多學習、運用英文的機會，十年一定不白學。祝各位在學習完本書後，能流暢地在日常生活中使用英文，聽、說、讀、寫無一不能。

使用說明

顛覆傳統制式學習方法，
利用自身的菜英文，
循序漸進架構更好的能力，
英文輕鬆開口說！

01 暖身練習，重新找回使用英文的記憶！

學習前先來個輕鬆的小暖身，讓眼熟的英文，先重新啓動你記憶深處曾經學習過的英語，找回英文語感，並驗證是否熟悉這一類的英文，有利於克服學習恐懼、增加自信。請根據指示進行練習，爲接下來的學習做準備。

02 絕對學過只是遺忘！加強訓練單字、句型、文法

利用有趣的故事閱讀和適量MP3生活對話，從各種不同角度剖析每個主題，以聽力或閱讀測驗的方式來喚醒更多英文記憶，提高學習效率。題型涵蓋填空、選擇、判斷、搭配、填表格等，無論是單字、句型或文法，皆能充分訓練。

03 救回被遺忘的英文！延伸英文基礎概念，
　　再次復習，並更深入的學習。

有了基礎概念之後，學習者將在此部分對每個主題有更完整的認識。除了復習前面所學，也會再做延伸學習，例如：學習看懂家電的使用説明，描述自行車損壞的部位，在閱讀文章時學習修辭技巧，學著作筆記、分析文意、撰寫完整的句子和短文等。

04 你一定還想知道更多！

書中會不定時補充小知識，告訴學習者用字遣辭的差異和不同説法的細微變化，讓學習者從更細節處學習英文。

05 學習進度確認清單：學完這一單元，你就可以……

好不容易學習完一個單元了，快來檢查一下自己有沒有把該單元的重點完整掌握吧！若是確定自己都記住了，那就繼續接下來的作文練習；如果清單上有空著沒打勾的選項，務必要回頭再復習一遍！

06 讓你的英文能力起死回生！

要想學以致用，寫作是較好的訓練和驗證方式。因此，請在這個部分根據作者指示，將所學濃縮成一篇短文，別忘了要加入自己的想像力，讓文章看起來更多彩多姿。

07 單元總復習！

終於做完所有的練習了，相信你一定已經充分掌握該單元應該具備的能力了，不過，還是讓總復習的聽力測驗再幫助你彌補不足之處吧！此部分有表格填空和問答等題型，幫你快速回顧整個單元所學。

08 MP3音檔內容完整看！

每個單元都收錄了所有音檔的完整文字，除了讓學習者能找出自己聽錯的地方，加以注記之外，不熟的語彙要查辭典並作筆記，方能加深英文記憶。朗讀書本裡的對話文字，也是訓練口語的好方法，快來跟著讀讀看，你一定能說出一口發音漂亮的英文。

09 外師親錄強效學習MP3，
生活英語聽力口說同步訓練！

每個單元充份利用MP3內容，藉由反覆的收聽做測驗練習，不僅能加強聽力，同時更能跟著一起開口讀，訓練一口發音漂亮的口語。

目錄

Unit 1 家庭 The Family

Unit 2 家 The Home

Unit 3 日常事務 Daily Routines

Unit 4 出遊 Getting Around

Unit 1 家庭 The Family

Unit 1 家庭

The Family

在所有文化中，打招呼都是很重要的。我們要跟熟悉的人打招呼，有時候也需要與初次見面的人打招呼，或是與經由介紹而認識的人打招呼。有時候我們也需要自我介紹……那現在我就跟各位介紹一下自己吧！

 暖身練習，重新找回用英文自我介紹的記憶

Hello. Let me introduce myself.
My name's Gordon Guide.
Students call me Professor Guide.

假設我們現在是面對面的話，你會怎麼回應我呢？試試看，說出四到五個詞吧！大聲說出來，練習是很重要的。

回應完了以後，就換你自我介紹了。這對你來說應該不難吧！接下來你也會在音檔中聽到不同人物的自我介紹。

▶ 用大約四到五個詞回應作者之後，請試著自我介紹。

再做一個暖身練習，重新找回用英文打招呼的記憶

相信你應該也知道一些用英文打招呼的常見方式。下面有一些常見的用中文打招呼的方式，譯成英文大概是：

Lao Wang, where are you going?
（老王，你要去哪兒？）
Have you had breakfast?
（吃早餐了嗎？）
Have you bought some vegetables?
（買菜了嗎？）

如果你這樣和英文母語人士打招呼，他們應該會很驚訝！那應該怎麼跟他們打招呼才對呢？請試著在下面的橫線上寫下三到四句常見的英文打招呼用語！

▶ 寫下三到四句常見的英文打招呼用語。

_____

_____

_____

_____

 解題

Nice to meet you.
How are you?
Good morning.
How are things going?

Part 1——
10年英語不白學！
如何用英文自我介紹

　　現在準備聽一段對話，做做練習！在這段對話中，莎拉・布萊克帶了一位新朋友回到家，並把她介紹給家裡的其他人認識。

😃 絕對學過只是遺忘：人與人之間的關係怎麼說

　　聽對話，完成下面的表格。表格中的名字如果在對話中被提及，就在第二欄打個勾（√），如果沒有被提及則打個叉（X）。然後再聽聽所有被打勾的人和莎拉是什麼關係，在第三欄中寫下來。已經幫你做好一題當示範了！

🔊 將對話中提到的人名打勾，並寫出他們和莎拉的關係。 🔊 *Track 001*

Name of person	Mentioned (√) Not mentioned (×)	Relationship to Sara
Richard	√	her husband
Li Ting		
Zhong Weitao		
Val		
Helen		
Sam		
Tom		

😊 絕對學過只是遺忘：人與人之間的打招呼用語怎麼說

再聽一次剛才的對話，這次要注意每個說話人使用的語句，並填好以下的空格。

🔊 聽對話，在空格內填入適當的單字。 🔈 *Track 001*

ⓐ (Sara) Li Ting, <u>this</u> <u>is</u> Val, Valerie Edmunds, a very good friend of mine.

ⓑ (Val) _____, Li Ting. _____ _____ to meet you.

ⓒ (Li Ting) _____, er ... Val, _____ to meet you.

ⓓ (Sara) And _____ _____ Richard, my husband.

ⓔ (Richard) _____, Li Ting. _____ to the neighbourhood.

ⓕ (Li Ting) _____, Richard. _____ _____ to meet you.

🛸 解題

莎拉把李婷介紹給了四個人：她的丈夫理查德、她的好朋友瓦萊麗、她的兒子湯姆跟山姆。你在第一個練習的表格中都勾對了嗎？寫下這些人和莎拉的正確關係了嗎？一定有吧！對你來說，相信這不難。

第二個練習也沒有很難吧！在這個練習中，你會發現要介紹人們認識其實很簡單！只要說 This is ... （人名），就可以了。在這個人的名字後面，還可以再加上一些資訊，例如：這個人和你是什麼關係（my close friend 我的好朋友，my husband 我丈夫），或這個人是從哪裡來的（例如：all the way from China 從中國遠道而來）。

第二個練習中，你應該也寫下了以下這些回應：

(Val) I'm glad to meet you.

(Li Ting) Val, pleased to meet you.

(Li Ting) It's good to meet you.

這些都是很常見的回應，你想用哪個都可以。理查德則是說 Welcome to the neighbourhood.。這是回應拜訪者時非常有用的一句。你還可以說 Welcome to Taiwan.，Welcome to Taipei.，Welcome to our school. 等，視情況而定。但如果要說 You are welcome to ...，則不太適合。

在第二個練習的其他空格中，你填入的應該都是一些比較簡單的單字才對。像是常見的打招呼方式： Hi 或 Hello。

😀 絕對學過只是遺忘：如何從一段對話中聽出更多資訊

現在我們再來回想一下剛剛聽的對話，裡面究竟說了哪些內容？請在下面的題目中圈出正確的答案。

📢 圈出正確的答案。 🔊 *Track 001*

❶ The context of the conversation is _____.

    A. extremely formal

    B. formal

    C. informal

    D. very informal

❷ The name Val _____.

    A. is the short form of a first name

    B. is the full form of a first name

    C. is the short form of a family name

    D. is the full form of a family name

❸ Sara's children call Val _____.

    A. Val

    B. Valerie

    C. Mrs. Val

    D. Mrs. Edmunds

❹ Tom and Sam are _____.

    A. friends who look alike

    B. identical male twins

    C. boy and girl twins

    D. twins who do not look alike

解題

這個對話的情境很不正式，因為對話是發生在莎拉的家裡，說話者都是家人和好友。李婷第一次來到這個家中，我們大概聽得出來，莎拉應該很希望她能和她的家人打成一片。

Val其實是暱稱，完整的名字應該是Valerie。在非正式場合，英文使用者常會為人們取簡短的暱稱（無論大人或小孩都一樣）。舉例來說，Thomas的暱稱可以是Tom，Samual的暱稱可以是Sam。

莎拉的小孩都直接用暱稱叫Val，這是很不正式的。有些長輩會希望孩子們稱呼他們為Mr.（先生），Mrs.（女士、太太，用於已婚者），Miss（小姐，用於未婚者），Ms.（女士，無特別指出是否已婚），但也有些長輩很樂意讓晚輩直呼名諱或喊他們的暱稱。

湯姆與山姆是雙胞胎，而且長得一模一樣。我們是如何知道的呢？「雙胞胎」這點是因為莎拉在對話裡面提到過，而知道他們長得一模一樣，是因為莎拉說很少有人可以分得出他們兩個之間的差別。identical 的意思就是「一模一樣」，你之前認不認識這個單字呢？如果不認識，可以查辭典。

答案：❶ D; ❷ A; ❸ A; ❹ B

Part 2——
10年英語不白學！
正式與非正式的介紹用語

這個練習中會有不少聽力練習，你準備好了嗎？在前一個練習中，你已經聽過了一段對話，對話中介紹了打招呼用語，都是比較口語、不拘小節的非正式用法。在這個練習中則要聽六段很簡短的對話，有的比較正式，有的則比較口語。英文要說得道地，就要懂得正式用語與口語的不同說法。這樣你只要聽了別人的對話，就知道他們之間到底有多熟了。

 絕對學過只是遺忘：什麼樣的場合應該說什麼樣的話

聽音檔，共有六段對話，猜猜這些對話發生在哪裡。以下表格中列出了十個不同的地方，你覺得哪段對話適合在哪個場景發生，就把對話序號寫在對應地點的後面，最後在剩餘的空格中打叉（X）。已經幫你做好一題當示範了！

聽音檔，在適當的位置寫下對話的序號。 ◀ *Track 002*

Place	Conversation
at a bus stop	3
in a doctor's surgery	
at the post office	
in a shop	
at the front door of a house	
at a swimming pool	

續表

Place	Conversation
in an office	
at an airport	
outside an examination room	
at a party	

 解題

在判斷的時候，你有沒有發現可以幫助作答的線索呢？在對話1中，你可以聽到一個男人與一個女人在辦公室裡說話。對話2是在某人的家門前發生的（為什麼可以判斷是某人的家門前呢？因為女人請男人進來，並提到了她的孩子和孩子們的玩具）。對話3是在公車站發生的（有個年輕男性說他希望公車快點來）。對話4是在商店裡發生的（可以聽到兩個年輕女人在討論生日卡價格昂貴）。對話5是醫生和病人之間的談話，可見場景是醫生的診所。對話6是在聚會上發生的（說話者在討論食物）。因此，以上表格有四項沒有提到：at the post office（在郵局），at a swimming pool（在游泳池中），at an airport（在機場），outside an examination room（在考場外面）。

 絕對學過只是遺忘：如何分辨正式對話和非正式對話

再聽一次這六段對話，並作筆記。請寫下：

a) 各段對話是正式的還是非正式的？

b) 各段對話中，說話者之前有沒有見過面？他們是陌生人還是他們聽說過對方，但之前沒見過面呢？

如果沒辦法確定答案，就寫個問號（？）吧！已經為你做好一題當範例了！

為這些對話記下筆記。 ◀ *Track 002*

Conversation 1

ⓐ business-like/professional/formal

ⓑ have heard of each other but never met

Conversation 2

ⓐ _____

ⓑ _____

Conversation 3

ⓐ _____

ⓑ _____

Conversation 4

ⓐ _____

ⓑ _____

Conversation 5

ⓐ _____

ⓑ _____

Conversation 6

ⓐ _____

ⓑ _____

解題

可以聽出來，對話1和5中說話者之間的關係很正式。其他的對話則比較口語，說話者之間的關係很友善。即使是像對話3和6中，說話者彼此不認識，但說話的語氣還是不太正式。一般在工作場合或看醫生的時候，需要用比較正式的詞語。對話1和2中的說話者不曾見過面，但聽說過對方。對話4中的說話者彼此是朋友。至於對話5，到底這個醫生和這個病人有沒有見過面，我們光聽對話無法判斷。

 絕對學過只是遺忘：如何挑選適當的方式和人打招呼

現在來仔細看看這些對話中使用的語言吧！請回答以下問題。如果需要，可以再聽一次音檔。

🔊 圈出最好的答案。 🔊 *Track 002*

❶ "How do you do?" is used _____.
   A. to greet an old friend
   B. when you meet someone for the first time in a formal context
   C. when you meet someone for the first time in an informal context
   D. to greet a person you already know but with whom you have a professional relationship

❷ "Hi." and "Hello." are used as greetings _____.
   A. only with people you know very well
   B. only when you meet a person for the first time in an informal context
   C. in any informal context — even when you have never met the person before
   D. when you meet a person for the first time in a formal context

❸ "Good morning.", "Good afternoon." and "Good evening." are used _____.

A. only between total strangers

B. between close friends

C. in formal contexts with people you already know

D. in formal contexts with both strangers and people you already know

❹ "Pleased to meet you." is used _____.

A. when you see an old friend

B. when you greet someone with whom you have a professional relationship

C. when you meet someone for the first time in a professional context

D. in both formal and informal contexts when you meet someone for the first time

❺ "How are you?" is used _____.

A. only when you see a close friend

B. when you see a person you know personally or professionally

C. when you meet someone for the first time in a formal context

D. when you meet someone for the first time in an informal context

---

🧪 解題

以上這個練習，就是要你熟悉一些最常見的打招呼的方式。自我介紹的時候，無論是在正式或非正式的場合，都可以說：I'm ...（我是……）；回應人家的自我介紹時，無論是在正式或非正式的場合，都可以說：Pleased to meet you.（很高興見到你。）在正式的場合，可以說：How do you do?（你好嗎？）但只能在初次見面的時候說。如果是面對已經認識的人，可以先說：Good morning（早安）或 Good afternoon（午安），Hello（你好），Hi（嗨），再問：How are you?（你好嗎？）Good morning 和 Good afternoon 都是比較正式的說法，對陌生人或已經認識的人都可以用。

答案：❶ B; ❷ C; ❸ D; ❹ D; ❺ B

Part 3——
10年英語不白學！
美式與英式英文中服飾的說法

　　你可能已經知道很多服裝款式的英文怎麼說了。不過，有趣的是，隨著時代的變化，服裝款式也會跟著改變。在這個練習中，希望你可以學到一些新的服裝款式，也許你還會改變對於一些已知的服飾名稱的理解。

😀 絕對學過只是遺忘：如何正確地描述服飾

　　以下題目中，都是講服裝款式的單字。每個單字都少一些字母，你能不能把這些字母填出來呢？下面有對照的中文意思可以參考。

Q 將這些單字補充完整。

❶ c _ _ t	❼ sw _ _ tshirt	⓭ dr _ ss	⓳ t _ _ sh _ _ t
❷ sh _ _ s	❽ j _ _ ns	⓮ _ _ orts	⓴ v _ _ t
❸ tr _ _ _ _ rs	❾ sw _ _ t _ r	⓯ sn _ _ k _ _ s	
❹ sk _ t	❿ car _ _ _ _ n	⓰ j _ c _ t	
❺ sh _ _ t	⓫ p _ _ ts	⓱ sunh _ t	
❻ tr _ _ n _ rs	⓬ bl _ _ se	⓲ c _ p	

❶ 外套	❺ 襯衫	❾ 毛衣	⓭ 洋裝	⓱ 遮陽帽
❷ 鞋子	❻ 運動跑鞋	❿ 開襟羊毛衫	⓮ 短褲	⓲ 帽子
❸ 長褲	❼ 運動長袖衫	⓫ 運動長褲	⓯ 運動鞋	⓳ T恤
❹ 短裙	❽ 牛仔褲	⓬ 女式襯衫	⓰ 夾克	⓴ 背心

解題

① coat; ② shoes; ③ trousers; ④ skirt; ⑤ shirt; ⑥ trainers; ⑦ sweatshirt; ⑧ jeans; ⑨ sweater; ⑩ cardigan; ⑪ pants; ⑫ blouse; ⑬ dress; ⑭ shorts; ⑮ sneakers; ⑯ jacket; ⑰ sunhat; ⑱ cap; ⑲ tee shirt; ⑳ vest

關於服飾的單字會有一些問題，比如明明是同一種服飾，英式英文和美式英文用的單字可能不太一樣。更麻煩的是，有時候明明是不同的服飾，英式英文和美式英文卻會用同一個單字！在下一個練習中，你會了解更多這方面的細節。

絕對學過只是遺忘：trousers 跟 pants 到底有什麼差別

讀讀下面這篇刊登在一本美國雜誌中的文章吧！作者是一位住在倫敦的美國商人。從標題看，你應該就猜得到這篇文章是在講服飾吧！先來看看第一段。

Q 讀第一段。

看完第一段，你會發現這篇文章探討的是英式與美式英文使用的辭彙差異。我們來看看作者到底在說什麼吧！快速把整篇文章掃過一遍，將所有的服飾單字都畫上底線。

Q 將文章中所有表示服飾的單字畫上底線。

Am I safe in my vest and pants?

I love London but I am beginning to wonder if the people here really speak the same language as we speak in the States. It's usually fine when we're talking about politics, but as soon as we start to talk about something basic like things at home (in the apartment ... or, as they say, flat!), things to do with cars, food or clothes, I have problems.

Let's take clothes as an example. Sure, we all — British or American — wear coats, jackets, shirts, shoes and jeans but there are problems when it comes to sneakers. I went into a shoe store the other day to buy a pair of sneakers. The clerk looked at me blankly. "You know," I said, "comfortable sports shoes — the type that everyone wears these days." "Oh, you mean trainers," she replied. So, I bought a pair of trainers. Or are they sneakers?

The British call pants "trousers" — and that's fine. Few Americans have problems with that word! But, can you believe it, for the British "pants" are what we call underwear, shorts or slip. There's a similar problem with the word "vest" too. While we Americans wear our vests over our shirts and under our suit jackets, the British wear their vests under their shirts. Yes, a vest for the British is another item of underwear. An American vest is a waistcoat for the British! The problem does not stop here. We guys in the States use suspenders to hold up our trousers. British men use braces for the same purpose. Suspenders in Britain are used by a few sexy women — to hold up their stockings!

I haven't yet made any serious mistakes — that I know about! But, male Americans, just remember, never talk about your vest and pants to a British lady!

 解題

有很多單字要畫上底線吧！以下這些單字你都畫出來了嗎？如果現在你不知道它們的意思也不用擔心，接下來就會學到了。

coats, jackets, shirts, shoes, jeans, sneakers, sports shoes, trainers, pants, trousers, underwear, shorts, slip, vest, waistcoat, suit jackets, braces, suspenders, stockings

😃 絕對學過只是遺忘：美式與英式英文中的「服飾」有哪些不同的地方

現在就利用文章中的資訊，在這些圖片的下面寫下它們的「美式英文」（American English，*AmE*）和「英式英文」（British English，*BrE*）的說法吧！

A.

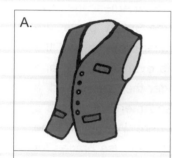

AmE: *vest*

BrE: *waistcoat*

B.

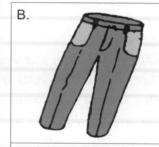

AmE:

BrE:

C.

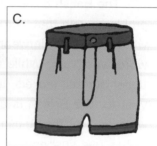

AmE:

BrE:

D.

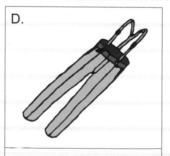

AmE:

BrE:

E.

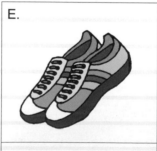

AmE:

BrE:

解題

答案：圖B：pants（美式），trousers（英式）
　　　圖C：underwear或shorts或slip（美式），pants（英式）
　　　圖D：suspenders（美式），braces（英式）
　　　圖E：sneakers（美式），trainers（英式）

請注意，在英文中，有很多服飾單字一般而言都是複數，例如：trousers（長褲），pants（長褲），shoes（鞋子），trainers（運動鞋）。這些東西都是成對的，或者包含兩個一模一樣的部分。這些複數單字前面也可以加上a pair of，不過大部分人都懶得加，也就是說，我們可能會經常聽到I bought some trainers.，而不是I bought a pair of trainers.。兩種說法都是正確的。

另外，sweater，pullover，jumper 這三個單字的意思都差不多，都是毛衣的意思。有些人會比較喜歡說sweater，有些人會比較喜歡說pullover或jumper，都一樣，都是羊毛的衣服！還有一種cardigan也是羊毛做的，但它們的前面有扣子，穿的方式跟外套一樣，不像sweater，pullover，jumper 是直接用套的方式穿上去。

至於sweatshirt，看起來可能跟sweater有點像，不過通常不是羊毛做的，而是綿布做的，而且看起來比較「運動風」。

以上提到的所有服飾類單字，你都會了嗎？在前面的那篇文章中，就說明了許多服飾類單字的意思了。如果還有哪些單字不清楚，可以翻開辭典查看或上網搜尋圖片！

Part 4—
10年英語不白學！
花紋、設計與風格

　　還記得前面對話中出現過的雙胞胎，湯姆跟山姆嗎？因為他們長得一模一樣，所以要分清楚他倆是很困難的。因此，他們的媽媽莎拉就常鼓勵他們穿稍微不太一樣的衣服，譬如說一個人穿紅色的T恤，另一個人穿藍色的；或一個人穿格子襯衫，另一個人穿條紋的。現在的衣服有很多種不同的材質，例如：wool（羊毛），cotton（綿質），nylon（尼龍），denim（牛仔布），silk（絲），acrylic fabric（人造合成布料）等。你不需要把這些布料的名稱都背下來，不過關於服飾的花紋怎麼說，還是應該學一下。

 絕對學過只是遺忘：花紋與圖案怎麼說

以下這些單字形容的是不同的花紋與圖案。

striped　　spotted　　checked　　flowered　　plain

with stars　　with an abstract design　　with a geometric pattern

把這些單字與以下的圖片搭配起來。我已經為你寫好了一題當作範例！

Q　在每張圖片下面寫下適當的單字。

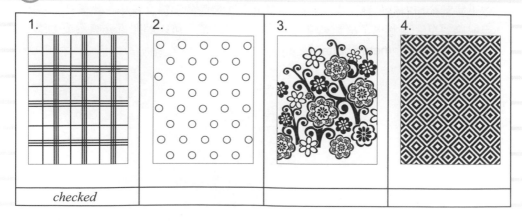

1. *checked*
2.
3.
4.

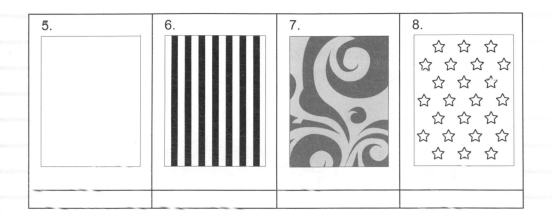

解題

答案：2. spotted; 3. flowered; 4. with a geometric pattern; 5. plain; 6. striped;
7. with an abstract design; 8. with stars

　　想像一下你四周的人穿的衣服，有沒有人穿普通單色、格子或條紋的衣服呢？有沒有人穿有花的洋裝或有圖案的短裙呢？你有沒有上面這種抽象或幾何圖形的服裝呢？你有沒有上面這種星星圖案的服裝呢？

請注意這些說明花紋的單字的位置：

我們會說：a flowered dress （flowered在dress的前面）

但碰到比較長的修飾語時，要這樣表達：a dress with a geometric pattern
（with a geometric pattern在dress 的後面）

　　也就是說，flowered，plain，striped 等都是形容詞，所以會放在名詞的前面；至於with stars，with a geometric pattern 這些比較長的說法則會放在名詞的後面。請注意，如果我們參加聚會，想問清楚誰是誰，就可以這樣說：

Who is the man <u>wearing</u> the grey sweater? （那個穿灰色毛衣的男人是誰？）
也可以說：
Who is the man <u>in</u> the grey sweater?

😊 絕對學過只是遺忘：如何準確描述髮型

如何分出誰是誰？除了看衣服以外，當然還可以看頭髮。頭髮是外表很重要的一部分，我們常會討論頭髮長短、髮色、髮型等。

看看下面的圖片，試著把這些圖片與以下這些形容搭配起來。我已經為你做好第一題了！

ⓐ She has short, curly hair.
ⓑ She has (her hair in) plaits.
ⓒ She has medium length, wavy hair.
ⓓ She has (her hair in) a bun.
ⓔ She has long, straight hair.
ⓕ She has (her hair in) a pony tail.
ⓖ She has short hair and a fringe.
ⓗ He has a crew cut.

Ⓠ 在每張圖片旁邊寫下正確的句子編號。

1. ⓔ   2.   3.   4.

5.   6.   7.   8.

解題

對你來說，這些形容詞應該有的很簡單，有的比較難一點吧！

答案：2. **f** ; 3. **c** ; 4. **a** ; 5. **d** ; 6. **b** ; 7. **h** ; 8. **g**

你一定還想知道更多！

請注意，我們除了可以說：She/He has short hair/a bun/a crew cut. 之外，也可以說：

The girl with short, curly hair ...
The man with a crew cut ...
The woman with a bun ...

所以，我們可以問：
Who is the lady <u>that has</u> long dark hair?

也可以問：
Who is the lady <u>with</u> long dark hair?

順帶一提，你知不知道lady和woman兩者之間的差別呢？它們都可以用來指成年女性，但lady是對對方比較尊敬一些的稱呼，尤其是在英國。

在形容髮型的時候，美式跟英式英文也是有差別的！上面所用的所有說法都是英式英文。舉例來說，英式英文會用a fringe表示「瀏海」，美式英文則會說bangs。英式英文會用plaits表示「辮子」，美式英文則會說braids。

Part 5——
讓你的英文能力起死回生！
學學怎麼描述照片裡的這些人

　　這次的練習又要聽音檔了，準備好了嗎？你會聽到兩個人分別在描述一張照片，先講話的人是莎拉，另一個人是李婷。她們兩個正在拿這張照片給朋友們看。

😊 救回被遺忘的英文：如何描述人們身上的服裝

　　聽聽莎拉和李婷對照片中人物的描述，把下面的Clothing（服裝）欄填好。現在先不用填Position（位置）和Appearance（外表）兩欄。請注意，這段對話中不是每個人的服裝都被提到，所以有幾欄不填也沒關係。我已經為你填好第一行了！

🔊 聽音檔，在Clothing欄作筆記。　🔈*Track 003*

Name	Position	Clothing	Appearance
Sara	in the middle	long-sleeved, checked dress	
Richard			
Sara's mum			
Sara's dad			
Li Ting			
Val			
Tim			
Helen			
Danny			
Tom			
Sam			

救回被遺忘的英文：如何描述人們的位置與外表

　　再聽一次音檔，把表格的另外兩欄（Position，Appearance）填好吧！要描述位置的時候，可以使用一或兩個介系詞片語，像在範例中，我就寫下了in the middle（在中間）。而要描述外表時，可以寫下髮型、身高、身材等。對話中並不是每個人的外表都提到了，所以有些空格可以不填。

 聽音檔，在上頁的表格中作筆記，記錄下每個人的位置和外表。
◀Track 003

解題

Name	Position	Clothing	Appearance
Sara	in the middle	long-sleeved, checked dress	
Richard	behind Sara	jeans and a tee shirt	tall guy with short, dark hair
Sara's mum	under the tree, on the left	flowered dress	plump
Sara's dad	on the right		with white hair and a moustache
Li Ting	beside Sara's mum	silk dress with tiny stars	
Val		jeans and a checked shirt	with short wavy hair
Tim			
Helen		short skirt and spotted blouse	straight, blond hair
Danny		striped shirt	
Tom		shorts and a striped tee shirt	
Sam		shorts and a plain tee shirt	

救回被遺忘的英文：如何正確指出「誰是誰」

現在你是不是可以利用你填好的表格，認出照片裡誰是誰了呢？把正確的字母寫在下面的表格中。

Q 對照圖片，在每個人的名字旁邊寫下適當的字母。

	Name	Letter
1	Sara	
2	Richard	
3	Sara's mother	
4	Sara's father	
5	Li Ting	
6	Val	
7	Helen	
8	Tim (Val's son)	

續表

	Name	Letter
9	Danny	
10	Tom	
11	Sam	

解題

是不是有點複雜呢？你認出誰是誰了嗎？快來看看答案。

答案：1. H; 2. K; 3. F; 4. A; 5. E; 6. J; 7. G; 8. B; 9. D; 10. C; 11. I

救回被遺忘的英文：如何從圖片中獲得更多資訊

32頁的表格中，還有一些空格你填不出來對不對？因為對話裡都沒講到啊！幸好現在你可以看著這張圖片，把剩下的空格填完，因為每個人的服裝、髮型等都可以從圖片中看得清清楚楚了。

Q 利用圖片完成32頁的表格。

救回被遺忘的英文：如何完成每個人的簡介

讀讀以下每個人的簡介，並在空格處填入圖片中對應的那個人。

Q 寫下以下描述的人名。

A _____ is in the middle of the photo, standing behind Sam. She is wearing a long-sleeved checked dress.

B _____ is on the right of the photo, standing beside Tom. He's wearing jeans and a short-sleeved plain shirt.

C _____ is on the left of the photo, sitting under the tree. She is quite plump with short curly hair. She's wearing a flowered dress.

D _____ is in the middle of the photo, lying in front of the whole group. He has a crew cut. He's wearing a striped shirt and sneakers.

解題

相信這一定難不倒你吧！

答案：**A** Sara; **B** Tim; **C** Sara's mum; **D** Danny

救回被遺忘的英文：如何簡單地描述每個人

現在換你說了！參考上個練習中的句子，各用三句話描述莎拉的父親，瓦萊麗和山姆。你可以先把這些描述寫在筆記本上，然後大聲說出來。

Sara's father _____

Val _____

Sam _____

救回被遺忘的英文：描述照片或圖片時，要使用現在進行式

在上個練習中，你寫下的句子是否都使用了現在進行式呢？一定要使用現在進行式！這是因為我們在看照片或描述圖片時，會說得好像照片中的人就在現場，而且他們做的動作都是「現在」正在做的樣子。舉例來說，莎拉在描述李婷時，說：She is wearing a gorgeous silk dress with tiny stars.（她穿了一件漂亮的絲質洋裝，上面有小星星。）但在聽音檔時，你可能會發現莎拉也用了一般現在式。莎拉在描述她老公的時候就說：He usually wears glasses...（他總是戴著眼鏡。），而在描述瓦萊麗時，則說：...always wears casual clothes...（她總是穿著休閒服裝。）這些都是用一般現在式，用來描述一些「一般而言總是在發生」的事情。舉例來說，瓦萊麗一般總是穿著休閒服裝，在這張照片裡也是，就可以說：Val is wearing casual clothes in the photo and she always wears casual clothes. 而理查德一般總是戴著眼鏡，但在這張照片裡沒戴，則可以說：Richard is not wearing glasses in the photo but he usually wears them.

現在來看看下面的句子（都是使用一般現在式），並聽聽音檔，判斷哪些句子是事實，哪些不是。在正確的句子旁邊把T（True）圈起來，在不正確的句子旁邊把F（False）圈起來。如果句子不正確，要把它改寫成正確的。第一題已經為你填好了！

🔊 聽音檔，確定以下句子是否正確。不正確的要改正過來。 🔈 *Track 003*

❶ Richard wears jeans for work.   T   Ⓕ

Richard wears a suit and tie for work.

❷ Richard usually wears glasses.   T   F

❸ Danny never wears sneakers for work.   T   F

❹ The twins wear grey trousers and white shirts for picnics.   T   F

❺ Val usually wears silk dresses.   T   F

❻ Li Ting occasionally joins the Black family when they
have gatherings. T F

❼ Tim often plays tricks on people. T F

解題

只有第**❷**題是正確的！其他幾句都要改寫才行！

第**❸**題改成：Danny *always* wears sneakers for work.

第**❹**題改成：The twins wear grey trousers and white shirts for *school.*

第**❺**題改成：Val usually wears *casual clothes.*

第**❻**題改成：Li Ting *often* joins the Black family when they have gatherings.

第**❼**題改成：*The twins* often *play* tricks on people.

你一定還想知道更多！

你都答對了嗎？順帶一提，occasionally的意思是not very often，也就是「不常」。

在第7題中，你把動詞由plays改成play了嗎？仔細想想，需要這樣改的理由是什麼呢？

其實是因為動詞現在式會受主詞影響，原本的主詞Tim是第三人稱單數，故用plays；句子改正後，主詞The twins是複數，並非第三人稱單數現在式，所以play不用加s。

 救回被遺忘的英文：介系詞的重要性

再完成一個簡單的練習，這個部分就結束了！下面有三個句子，把它們補充完整吧！這些句子你在剛才的音檔中都聽到過！

🔊 在空格內填入適當的單字。 🔊 *Track 003*

❶ It's quite a good one _____ everyone.

❷ This is a lovely photo _____ her.

❸ It's a terrible photo _____ me.

 解題

這三句到底少了哪個單字呢？我現在不直接告訴你，請你再聽聽音檔中的描述，就能找到答案了！不過你也可以看看下面這些句子該怎麼填，說不定會有靈感：

My mother likes me to send her photos so that she can see what my baby son looks like as he gets bigger, so I often take photos _____ my son to send to my mother. The photos are *for* my mother (but _____ my son).

You have a camera and would like to take a photo to remind you of your American friend who is leaving China. What would you say to him/her?

Do you mind if I take a photo _____ you?

（請注意，我在以上的句子中，說了photo而沒用 photograph。這是因為photo是photograph的簡短說法，現在大家都普遍使用了！）

答案：❶ of; ❷ of; ❸ of

Part 6——
讓你的英文能力起死回生！
如何維持人與人之間的互動關係

現在你對莎拉一家人應該很了解了吧！在這個活動中，你會聽到更多關於他們的事。下面聽到的這個對話發生在他們家的廚房裡。

☺ 救回被遺忘的英文：如何描述你們家的晨間時光

聽對話，你將會知道莎拉一家人每天早上都做些什麼事。在聽對話前，可以先想像一下你自己的家庭，你們每天早上都做些什麼呢？把每天早上家裡會做的重要事項都寫在下面，請至少寫六項。我已經為你寫好第一項（也是最理所當然的一項）了！

Ｑ 寫下你們家人早上會做哪些重要的事。

getting up,

解題

我無法判斷你寫的對不對，因為我也不知道你們一家人早上都會做些什麼事。但你是不是提到了brushing teeth（刷牙），washing（盥洗），dressing（穿衣服），eating（吃東西），drinking（喝東西）？大部分人都會在早上做這些事吧？

救回被遺忘的英文：早上會做哪些事情

以下列舉了一些早上可能會做的事。聽聽對話，若對話中有提到的事情就打個勾吧！

聽音檔，在提到過的活動後打勾（✓）。 *Track 004*

1 getting up _____
2 making beds _____
3 having a shower _____
4 getting dressed _____
5 doing some exercise _____
6 cooking breakfast _____
7 washing the dishes _____
8 having breakfast _____
9 talking about the weather _____
10 listening to the radio _____
11 reading a newspaper _____
12 discussing weekend plans _____
13 discussing shopping _____
14 waking up other family members _____

解題

莎拉一家人做的事跟你家的像不像呢？應該有些相似之處吧！不過，你們家每天早上會討論周末要做什麼嗎？說不定會。但你們會邊吃早餐邊討論你老公的前妻或你老婆的前夫嗎？好像不會吧。相信你從這段對話中，可以感受到西方國家與東方國家家庭關係的一些不同之處。

答案：**1**, **3**, **6**, **8**, **9**, 10, 12, 14 需要打勾。

☺ 救回被遺忘的英文：如何描述人與人之間的親屬關係

相信你應該學過以下這些親屬稱謂的說法了：

mother   father   son   daughter   sister   brother
aunt   uncle   grandmother   grandson

那接下來這些親屬稱謂你知道嗎？

ex-husband   cousin   stepmother   father-in-law
natural mother   stepson   sister-in-law   niece
nephew   fiancée   fiancé

讀讀接下來這些句子，從上面這些單字或片語中挑出最正確的填入空格中。遇到問題的話，可以翻辭典查查看！我已經做好第一題當範例了！

Ⓠ 把空格填好。

❶ Her <u>fiancé</u> is the man to whom she is engaged to be married.

❷ His _____ is the woman to whom he is engaged to be married.

❸ Her/His _____ is the woman who gave birth to her/him.

❹ My _____ is the son of my sister or brother, or the son of my wife's/husband's sister or brother.

❺ My _____ is the daughter of my sister or brother, or the daughter of my wife's/husband's sister or brother.

❻ My _____ is my father's wife in a second or later marriage.

❼ My _____ is the son of my husband/wife but not my natural son.

❽ My _____ is my husband's/wife's father.

❾ My _____ is the man I used to be married to but whom I am now divorced.

❿ My _____ is my husband's/wife's sister or my husband's/wife's brother's wife.

⓫ The son or daughter of my aunt or uncle is my _____.

解題

現在就來看看你答得如何吧！第二題的答案是 fiancée。 fiancé 和 fiancée 都是從法文演變過來的，所以念法也很特別。雖然這兩者拼法不同，但念起來卻是一樣的。其他的答案是： ❸ natural mother; ❹ nephew; ❺ niece; ❻ stepmother; ❼ stepson; ❽ father-in-law; ❾ ex-husband; ❿ sister-in-law; ⓫ cousin

😄 救回被遺忘的英文：學習準確地說出親屬關係

現在我們已經學了這麼多種親屬關係的說法，就換你來猜猜看莎拉一家人彼此之間到底是什麼關係吧！看起來簡單，但其實不見得喔！聽對話，填入以下的空格。

🔊 聽對話，填好空格。 🔊 *Track 004*

❶ Helen is Sara's <u>stepdaughter</u>.

❷ Alice is Helen's _____.

❸ Sara is Richard's _____.

❹ Richard is Mary and Henry's _____.

❺ Henry is Tom and Sam's _____.

❻ Alice is Richard's _____.

❼ Mary and Henry are Sara's _____.

❽ Helen is Mary and Henry's _____.

解題

你一開始是不是覺得莎拉是海倫的生母呢？聽到理查德說She's spending Friday night with her mother.的時候，是不是嚇了一跳呢？其實艾麗斯才是海倫的生母（natural mother）！

其他的解答如下：❸ wife (or second wife); ❹ son; ❺ grandfather; ❻ ex-wife; ❼ parents-in-law; ❽ granddaughter

😀 救回被遺忘的英文：如何從一段對話中聽出重要的資訊

現在你知道莎拉一家人的關係多複雜了吧！你還知道他們每天早上都做些什麼事。接下來，我們來聽聽這段對話中還有什麼有用的資訊。試著回答下面的這些問題吧！

🔊 回答以下問題（只需要用幾個單字即可）。　◀*Track 004*

❶ Where is the washing drying?

❷ Why can't Sara hang the washing outside to dry?

❸ Who disturbs Richard?

❹ Why does Richard need to go back to sleep?

❺ When is Richard's mother arriving?

❻ When is Richard's father arriving?

解題

1 In the house. **2** It's raining. **3** The boys.
4 Because he came home very late last night.
5 On Friday evening.
6 On Saturday evening.

😊 救回被遺忘的英文：如何描述一個人的個性與態度

從對話中，可以聽出一些家庭成員的個性與態度。把下面正確的選項圈出來吧！

🔊 聽音檔，將正確的選項圈出來，然後將音檔中能夠當作答案依據的句子寫在橫線上。 ◀ *Track 004*

1 A. The boys are well-behaved.

(B.) The boys make a lot of noise in the mornings.

C. The boys get up early.

The boys always cause trouble in the mornings.

2 A. Alice is "an angel".

B. Alice is a bad person.

C. Alice is sometimes rather selfish.

_____

3 A. Sara is rather jealous of Alice because she's Helen's natural mother.

B. Sara is rather jealous because Alice used to be married to Richard.

C. Sara is rather jealous because Helen loves Richard more than her.

❹ A. Helen is rather naughty compared with her brothers.

B. Helen is jealous of her brothers.

C. Helen is well-behaved compared with her brothers.

❺ A. Richard is not interested in his sons.

B. Richard is not kind enough to his sons.

C. Richard is not strict enough with his sons.

解題

❷ C (She is just a bit selfish at times.)

❸ A (I'm still a bit jealous that she's Helen's real mother.)

❹ C (She's such an angel compared with our two boys.)

❺ C (You spoil them.)

這裡順便提一下spoil這個字。這個字是什麼意思呢？就是「寵壞」的意思。
比如你的孩子們要什麼你就給什麼，你就是spoil them。

😊 救回被遺忘的英文：學會用拋出問題的方式繼續進行對話

現在我們就來看看對話中常用的句型吧！你可能還記得，在對話開始的時候，莎拉正在跟海倫討論天氣。海倫說：It's really depressing, isn't it?（這天氣好令人憂鬱，對不對？）你真的覺得這是個問題嗎？的確，後面有個問號，但我們大概都看得出來，海倫並不是真的想問莎拉這天氣有沒有很令人憂鬱。明明沒有疑問，卻還是問了問題，這其實是聊天中常用的一個方式。我們其實已經知道對方對某事的看法了，根本不需要問他們問題，但還是使用了問句，這樣對方就必須回答這個問題，對話才能繼續進行下去。

"... isn't it?" 這種形式在英文中叫做 "question tag"（疑問句尾）。海倫講了一個肯定句（It's really depressing），但卻加上了一個否定的疑問句尾（isn't it?）。她預期得到的答案是肯定的，果然莎拉就說了 Yes。至於否定句，後面則是一般加肯定的疑問句尾。舉例來說，如果海倫說：It's not very pleasant, is it?（這天氣不怎麼好，對不對？），這時，對方通常應該回答No。

在這段對話中，還有六個這樣的反意疑問句例子。聽對話，完成下面的句子。

🔊 聽音檔，寫下其中的反意疑問句。 🔈 *Track 004*

❶ The boys always cause trouble in the mornings, don't they?

❷ _____

❸ _____

❹ _____

❺ _____

❻ _____

解題

答案： **2** Helen should be back by then, shouldn't she?

3 Alice isn't that bad, is she?

4 But Helen adores you, doesn't she?

5 That's them now, isn't it?

6 You'd also love to stay in bed these days, wouldn't you?

救回被遺忘的英文：如何運用反意疑問句拋出問題

　　從上面的範例你應該可以看出來，在疑問句尾中使用的動詞時態，都和陳述句本身時態相同。如果陳述句是一般過去式的句子，疑問句尾中就要搭配使用did或be動詞的過去式，如果是一般現在式的句子，則要搭配使用do, does或be動詞的現在式。現在就練習將下面的句子加上疑問句尾吧！注意，否定句後面要加肯定的疑問句尾，肯定句後面要加否定的疑問句尾，並將主詞改為代名詞。

Q 請將以下的句子填上疑問句尾。

1 Helen often visits her mother, _____?

2 Richard's parents are coming over at the weekend, _____?

3 The boys don't like getting up early, _____?

4 Richard shouldn't be so kind to the boys, _____?

5 Henry plays golf, _____?

6 Sara loved to stay in bed when she was young, _____?

7 He has finished his homework, _____?

8 It's not a difficult task, _____?

解題

答案： **1** doesn't she; **2** aren't they; **3** do they; **4** should he;
5 doesn't he; **6** didn't she; **7** hasn't he; **8** is it

Part 7——
讓你的英文能力起死回生！
回想以往的經歷並描述出來

從小到大，你有哪些改變呢？相信你的長相可能改變了，但個性呢？回想一個你從小就認識的人，例如某個家人或好友。你還記得你們小時候是如何一起玩的嗎？你們有多了解對方呢？現在你們都長大了，是不是更了解對方了呢？

☺ 救回被遺忘的英文：如何形容自己的個性

想像一下你小時候的個性，並回想一個你從小就認識的朋友。你當年是怎樣的人呢？在那個從小就認識的朋友眼中，你又是怎麼樣的人呢？填好下面的表格吧！

如果你或你的朋友覺得你符合左欄的敘述，就請你在YES處打個勾（√）。如果你或你的朋友覺得你不符合左欄的敘述，就請你在NO處打個勾（√）。如果你還真想不出來到底符不符合，那就在YES處畫個問號。

When I was a child ...	My opinion		My friend's opinion	
	YES	NO	YES	NO
I cried a lot.				
I was naughty.				
I was selfish.				
I was neat and tidy.				
I was happy.				

現在想像一下，身為大人的你，是個怎樣的人呢？不但要寫下自己的看法，也要寫下那位認識你很久的朋友的看法！

These days ...	My opinion		My friend's opinion	
	YES	NO	YES	NO
I am sociable.				
I am a responsible person.				
I am easy-going.				
I am shy.				
I am careless.				

解題

不知道你自己的看法與你家人或朋友的看法之間有沒有差異呢？從小到大，你是不是改變了不少呢？現在你應該準備好可以進行後面的練習了！

救回被遺忘的英文：如何從一篇文章中快速地抓到關鍵字並完成表格

接下來你將會讀到一篇名為 "Relative Opinions" 的文章。我們先來做一些練習，接下來再仔細地讀這篇文章。第一遍讀這篇文章的時候需要速讀，快速地抓住一些關鍵字，填好這個表格就可以！各個空格只需要填一或兩個詞彙。

Names of the two people	a. b.
Their relationship	
Who is older?	
What is their general attitude to each other? (positive or negative?)	

Relative Opinions

Sara Black and her older brother, Daniel Waterson (Danny), describe their lifelong relationship. They live ten minutes' drive from each other and see each other regularly.

Sara Black: My childhood was rather unusual. I lived with my parents and four brothers who were all much older than me. I was a "mistake": my parents didn't plan to have a fifth child. They were used to boys and then, when Danny, the youngest, was eight, I was born. Ours was always a noisy, untidy household and it was hard, at times, being the only girl. Everything at home seemed to be organised for the boys.

I realise now that the boys loved me, but when I was little I often felt lonely and left out. They were always having fun together, but I was too small to play with them. As a result, I suppose I was quite independent but I cried a lot because they used to play jokes on me and laugh at me so often. I always liked Danny more than my other brothers. He was kind and protective — as long as the others weren't around to stop him. All the boys had a great sense of humour — and Danny was especially funny — so I learned my sense of humour from them. I think they probably taught me to fight as well. At school, I was often described as aggressive and a bit of a "tomboy". The boys laughed at me whenever my mother dressed me in pretty dresses so I ended up wearing jeans or shorts all the time. And I still feel uncomfortable in very feminine and lady-like clothes.

I always wanted a big family myself. So I suppose I liked the busy atmosphere in my parents' house. I feel lucky to have Helen, my husband Richard's daughter from his first marriage, living with us. Female company is so special to me! Our own boys, Tom and Sam, are great and when I see them together, I'm reminded of my own brothers. I still hope to have more children. I think I've lost most of my old aggression and am quite gentle and easy-going these days. I sometimes think I'm too lenient with the children. I don't like punishing them.

We always have a house full of people. I'm very sociable and feel strange if ever I'm alone in the house. Danny and I are very similar in that way. He's still single but shares a house with four other people. He comes over here often too. The children love him. He's great fun and really patient — just like when I was little. We all love his sense of humour though occasionally I wish he would be more serious. He and I are still very close and I don't know what I'd do without him!

Daniel Waterson: When Sara was born, my brothers and I all pretended we weren't interested in her but she was such a wonderful addition to our family that we all learned to love her. For me, it was great to have someone younger around because I hadn't liked being the youngest. We all loved taking care of her so she was never alone. She was really spoiled — by Mum and Dad and all the boys. We gave her everything she wanted and she screamed and cried when she didn't have everyone's attention. She was a determined little girl and wanted to do everything for herself. But she was a real exhibitionist — always wanting to show us how well she could run, dance, jump and so on. Then she would get upset when we laughed at her. She had a great sense of humour though and is still very amusing.

I always thought she was selfish when we were kids but when I see her now with her own family I realise she's become very considerate and generous, always doing things for other people. I'm the selfish one! Sara's a great mother in most ways — but I sometimes feel she's a bit too strict with the boys. She's very relaxed and easy-going with Helen — which seems a bit unfair.

Sara's always trying to persuade me to settle down and have a family, but I'm happy just sharing hers at the moment. I think I'm good with children but I wouldn't make a very good husband — I'm much too irresponsible and disorganised. I'm sociable most of the time and love having fun with friends, but there are occasions when I'm quite anti-social and just want to shut myself away in my room with a good book and no interruptions.

I've always had good friends but very few girlfriends. I think I'm quite shy with women in some ways. In spite of my close relationship with Sara, I'm usually much more comfortable in male company — probably as a result of growing up in a male-dominated household. Having three older brothers gave me lots of confidence in the neighbourhood. I was proud to be one of the Waterson boys and I suppose I'm still rather confident these days, as a result. My brothers are still important to me but not quite so important as Sara.

解題

相信你應該很快就可以找到兩個主角的名字：莎拉・布萊克（Sara Black）與丹尼爾・沃特森（Daniel Waterson）。你應該也從簡介中發現了他們其實是兄妹吧！那他們對對方的態度如何呢？如果直接看一下每個人敘述的最後一句，應該就會發現他們很喜歡對方，對對方的態度也很正面。這裡給你 個根好用的提示：文章每段的第一句和最後一句通常都有很多實用的資訊！

文章的標題Relative Opinions其實是雙關語（pun）！也就是說它有兩種意思。relative可以是「親戚」的意思，也可以有「相對，比較」的意思，所以這篇文章的標題可以是「親戚們對對方的看法」，也可以是「兩人對對方的相對看法」。

救回被遺忘的英文：如何讀懂一篇文章並回答相關問題

看看下面這些敘述，再閱讀一遍上面的文章。下面這些敘述是正確的還是不正確的呢？如果是正確的，請把T（TRUE）圈起來，如果不正確，請把F（FALSE）圈起來，並把敘述改為正確的，將修改過後的敘述寫在下面橫線上。我已經為你做好第一題當作範例了！

Q 判斷以下敘述是否正確。錯誤的請改正。

❶ There were seven people in the Watersons' house before Sara was born.   T (F)

<u>There were six people in the Watersons' house before Sara was born.</u>

❷ Sara was the youngest of the four children.   T   F

_____

❸ Daniel was the youngest son in the family.   T   F

_____

❹ There is an eight-year age difference between Sara and Daniel.   T   F

_____

❺ Tom and Sam are Daniel's nephews.   T   F

_____

⑥ Helen is Tom and Sam's cousin.　　　　　　　　T　　F

_____

⑦ Richard is Daniel's brother-in-law.　　　　　　T　　F

_____

⑧ Daniel is married.　　　　　　　　　　　　　T　　F

_____

解題

答案：❷ F 改成：Sara was the youngest of the five children.
　　　❸ T
　　　❹ T
　　　❺ T
　　　❻ F 改成：Helen is Tom and Sam's sister (or half-sister).
　　　❼ T
　　　❽ F 改成：Daniel is single.

注意：海倫和湯姆與山姆有一個共同的生父，她就應該算是他們的half-sister 而不是stepsister。如果他們的生父、生母都不同，才能叫stepsister/ stepbrother。

救回被遺忘的英文：分析人們想表達的意見

　　現在我們再仔細看看莎拉與丹尼爾的意見吧！從文章中，你應該可以找出莎拉對她自己的看法，也可以找出丹尼爾對莎拉的看法。丹尼爾對莎拉的看法是否跟她對自己的看法一致呢？如果一致，就打個勾（√），如果不一致就畫個叉（X）。接下來，從文章中挑出和丹尼爾的意見相關的句子，來證明丹尼爾對莎拉的看法如何，並寫在第三欄。有點複雜，請仔細看看下面提供的範例！

Q 閱讀文章，並完成此表格。

	Sara's opinion:	Daniel agrees/ disagrees (√ or ×)	Daniel's opinion (and evidence):
1	I cried a lot.	√	She screamed and cried when she didn't have everyone's attention.
2	I felt lonely and left out because I was too small to play with the boys.		
3	All the boys had a great sense of humour and I learned it from them.		
4	I sometimes think I'm too lenient with the children.		

解題

2. × She was never alone.

3. √ She had a great sense of humour though and is still very amusing.

4. × I sometimes feel she's a bit too strict with the boys.

救回被遺忘的英文：分辨「正面」、「負面」或「中立」性質的形容詞

我們現在來看看文章裡面出現的一些單字吧！這是一篇充滿各種敘述的文章，所以也用了很多的形容詞。我們在形容自己或其他人、事、物時，都可能會表現出正面的（positive）、負面的（negative）、中立的（neutral）態度。有些形容詞一般而言都是正面的，也有一些形容詞一般而言都是負面的。但有些形容詞就很難判斷，要根據上下文才知道說話者到底是想表達正面還是負面的態度。舉例來說，請看看以下兩句話中的talkative一詞的用法。

(a) My roommate is very talkative so we have lots of interesting chats.

(b) The man sitting next to me on the train was very talkative so I couldn't read my book.

在(a)中，talkative的意思是正面的，但在(b)中則是負面的。

有時，也有可能用完全中立的方式使用形容詞，其中完全不包含正面或負面的態度。舉例來說：

(a) She's a very spontaneous person — always doing unexpected things.

(b) He's a very disciplined person who never does anything he hasn't planned.

在這兩句敘述中，我們沒辦法判斷spontaneous與disciplined到底是正面的還是負面的，因此需要更多的上下文才能作決定，所以我們只能說spontaneous和disciplined在這裡是「中立」的形容詞。

在文章中找出以下的這些敘述句，利用上下文和你對莎拉與丹尼爾的了解，判斷這些畫了底線的單字是正面（positive）、負面（negative）還是中立的（neutral）。

Q 讀文章，判斷以下畫底線的單字為正面、負面還是中立的。

❶ He was ... <u>protective</u>. ＿＿＿＿＿

❷ Daniel was especially <u>funny</u>. ＿＿＿＿＿

③ I was often described as <u>aggressive</u>. _____

④ I still feel uncomfortable in <u>feminine</u> ... clothes. _____

⑤ I ... am quite gentle and <u>easy-going</u> these days. _____

⑥ I'm too <u>lenient</u> with the children. _____

⑦ He's ... really <u>patient</u>. _____

⑧ He and I are still very <u>close</u>. _____

⑨ She was really <u>spoiled</u>. _____

⑩ (She) Is still very <u>amusing</u>. _____

⑪ I'm the <u>selfish</u> one. _____

⑫ I'm much too <u>irresponsible</u>. _____

⑬ There are occasions when I'm quite <u>anti-social</u>. _____

⑭ I think I'm quite <u>shy</u>. _____

⑮ I'm still <u>confident</u> these days. _____

解題

正面單字：❶ protective；❷ funny；❺ easy-going；❼ patient；❽ close；
❿ amusing；⑮ confident

負面單字：❸ aggressive；❻ lenient；❾ spoiled；⑪ selfish；⑫ irresponsible；
⑬ anti-social；⑭ shy

唯一一個「中立」的單字是❹（feminine）。莎拉並沒有說feminine的衣服到
底是好還是不好，只說她穿了覺得不太自在。

😃 救回被遺忘的英文：如何分辨意思正好相反的形容詞

　　這篇文章中有許多意思相反的詞。以下這些句子並非文章中的句子，每句都有一個畫了底線的形容詞。想一下這些形容詞的意思，並在文章中找找看，是否可以發現與其意思正好相反的形容詞呢？將意思相反的形容詞寫在每一句後面的橫線上。

Q 讀文章，找出與以下畫底線的單字意思相反的詞。

❶ My life these days is quite <u>ordinary</u>.　　　　　　　_____

❷ I am rather <u>ashamed</u> of my job.　　　　　　　_____

❸ My boss is a very <u>serious</u> guy.　　　　　　　_____

❹ His office is always extremely <u>neat</u>.　　　　　　　_____

❺ He is very <u>strict</u> with all his employees.　　　　　　　_____

❻ I think he's rather <u>selfish</u>.　　　　　　　_____

❼ His wife is surprisingly <u>shy</u> and seems afraid of everything.　　　_____

❽ She always seems <u>anxious</u>.　　　　　　　_____

❾ They seem to have a very <u>distant</u> relationship.　　　　_____

❿ It's a pity because everyone else in the office is very <u>sociable</u>.　_____

解題

答案：❶ unusual; ❷ proud; ❸ amusing/funny/easy-going; ❹ untidy;
　　 ❺ lenient; ❻ generous; ❼ confident; ❽ relaxed; ❾ close;
　　 ❿ anti-social

☺ 救回被遺忘的英文：運用still（仍然）來描述經驗

　　最後，我們再來看看這篇文章的語法吧！最常出現的動詞時態是什麼呢？很簡單吧！莎拉和丹尼爾用了很多次過去式（像是was、were、動詞+ed），因為他們提到很多過去的事，也用了不少現在式，因為他們在描述現在的狀態。

看看以下這些從文章中選取的例子：

I ended up wearing jeans or shorts all the time. And I still feel uncomfortable in very feminine ... clothes.
She had a great sense of humour and is still very amusing.

注意到still這個詞了嗎？它的用途是強調一件過去就已經在發生的事，到現在還是持續發生。現在來看看這句敘述：

I loved reading when I was a child and I still love reading now.

這個句子有好多重複，不夠漂亮。我們通常會改為：

I loved reading when I was a child and I still enjoy good books now.

試著使用**still**這個詞，改寫下面的句子吧！

Ⓠ 完成以下句子。

❶ I always hated spicy food when I was young and I _____.

❷ My mother was never selfish and she _____.

❸ I always enjoyed being with lots of people and I _____.

❹ My brother was never shy and he _____.

❺ _____ and I still like staying in bed in the mornings.

6 _____ and we still enjoy each other's company.

7 _____ and I still can't speak it very well.

8 _____ and I still practise as often as I can.

 解題

答案:

1 ... still dislike it now

2 ... is still very generous

3 ... am still sociable

4 ... is still confident these days

5 I never liked getting up early ...

6 We always spent a lot of time together ...

7 I always had problems with English ...

8 I played the piano when I was young ...

Part 8——
讓你的英文能力起死回生！
請試著寫出一篇作文

第一單元已經快結束了，你學得如何呢？下面列出了學完整個單元後應該具備的英語能力，希望這些能力學習者都能充分掌握。

 學完這一單元，你就可以：

☐ 在非正式場合自我介紹

☐ 在非正式場合介紹他人

☐ 討論家人之間的關係

☐ 找話題閒聊

☐ 形容外貌

☐ 形容個性

☐ 用說的或用寫的方式介紹自己

最後一項練習就是作文練習。請寫兩段，各約五六個句子，第一段的主題是你的孩童時代（你和誰一起住？你的個性如何？），而另一段的主題則是你現在的生活。你可以提到你想到的那位認識很久的朋友或家人，並寫下自己與他/她的關係。你可以從莎拉、丹尼爾的那篇訪談中尋找靈感，可以使用這個單元學到的形容詞，並寫下幾句用到still的句子。

請用I grew up in ...作為開頭。先在筆記本上寫下草稿，並檢查是否有錯。如果一切滿意，再抄寫到作業本上，可以拿給老師或其他人批改檢查。請把它的標題標為：

A Personal View

I grew up in _____

_____

_____

_____

_____

_____

_____

_____

_____

_____

_____

_____

_____

_____

_____

_____

總復習

 愛情仲介所

大衛去找所謂的愛情仲介所來替自己牽線，對方詢問了他理想對象的條件有哪些。

聆聽音檔，並將大衛的理想對象條件列在下方： ◀ *Track 005*

Age	
Educational Background	
Profession	
Appearance	
Personality	
Interests	

解題

Age	23—27
Educational Background	University degree, any subject
Profession	Private sector

Appearance	Under 1 metre 65, not too fat, not too thin, preferably long hair
Personality	A little ambitious, lively, sense of humour, kind, not selfish or greedy Not shy or lacking in self-confidence
Interests	Likes going out (restaurants, cafés, pubs), dancing, sport, particularly football and basketball Not someone who stays in

　　完成以上表格後，看看這些描述，與以下這些條件可能吻合的候選對象進行交叉比對，看看是否能為大衛找出一名理想的對象。也說不定沒有任何一個對象適合他！將你覺得適合的理由或不適合的理由列出。

Jessica

25 years old.

Degree in Music.

Musician for a privately-funded orchestra.

1 metre 60, very slim, with long hair. Quiet, studious, kind and generous.

Likes reading, listening to and playing music, and cooking.

Loves her job.

Linda

29 years old.

Teacher's Diploma.

Senior middle school teacher of English.

1 metre 58, slim, with long straight hair. Friendly, sociable, self-confident, good-humoured.

Loves dancing and singing.

Plays table tennis and swims regularly. Supports local football team.

Looking for a new job.

Catherine

27 years old.

Degree in Economics.

Salesperson for a Chinese-German joint venture.

1 metre 64, well-built, with shoulder-length hair. Very outgoing and lively, sometimes a little bossy.

Enjoys joking around with friends. Likes dancing, karaoke, going to films and theatre.

Hopes to become marketing manager eventually.

你覺得誰才是大衛的理想對象呢？

　　想必你一開始就把第一位候選人潔西卡和第二位候選人琳達給排除了，潔西卡個性安靜，和大衛又沒有共同的戶外運動愛好；而琳達在年齡上超過了大衛的理想年齡。第三位候選人凱瑟琳似乎很多條件都很理想，不在公家機關工作，而且她希望將來能成爲行銷主管，由此可見，凱瑟琳很有抱負，另外，她的外表完全符合條件，而且喜歡跳舞、不愛待在家，雖然似乎對運動不感興趣。不過還是值得一試嘛，説不定他們會相處愉快呢！

　　大功告成了嗎？那就準備進入第二個學習單元了！

MP3音檔內容完整看

若是聽完音檔還是沒把握，建議可搭配本部份學習，不熟的語彙要查辭典並作筆記，方能加深英文記憶。

 Part 1: Track 001　　（請配合014頁及音檔使用）

Sara: Hi, everyone! I'm home. And, look, I've brought Li Ting to meet you all. Remember? I told you about her. She's our new neighbour, all the way from China! Li Ting, this is Val, Valerie Edmunds, a very good friend of mine.

Val: Hi, Li Ting. I'm glad to meet you. Sara told me all about you.

Li Ting: Hello, er ... Val, pleased to meet you. Is it all right if I call you Val?

Val: Yeah, sure ... we're all very informal around here. Even Sara's children call me Val.

Sara: And this is Richard, my husband.

Richard: Hi, Li Ting. Welcome to the neighbourhood.

Li Ting: Hello, Richard. It's good to meet you.

Sara: And, Li Ting, here are my sons, the twins. This one's Sam and this is Tom. But, don't worry if you can't tell them apart. Few people can tell the difference between them ... and they just love to confuse everyone! Come on, boys, say "Hi" to Li Ting ...

 Part 2: Track 002　　（請配合018頁及音檔使用）

Conversation 1

Martha King: Good morning. Is this Mr. Fern's office? I'm looking for Mr. Fern.

Jasper Fern: That's me. How may I help you?

Martha King: Well, let me introduce myself. I'm Martha King and ...

Jasper Fern: Ah, Professor King! I've been expecting you. Jasper Fern. How do you do?

Martha King: Pleased to meet you, Mr. Fern.

Jasper Fern: Now, please, have a seat ... and let me take your coat.

Conversation 2

Sally: Hello?

Rod: Er, hello. I'm Rod, Rod Elston — Ken's friend from the factory.

Sally: Ah, of course. We've been expecting you. I'm Sally, Ken's wife.

Rod: Yes, I thought you might be. I'm happy to meet you at last.

Sally: Yes. I've heard of your name so many times. Anyway, please, come in, come in. Ken will be here in a moment. Excuse the toys. It's hard to keep the place tidy with young children at home all day!

Rod: Oh, don't worry about that. I'm used to it. We have two young ones as well ...

Conversation 3

Tim: Not exactly warm today, is it?

Gary: No ... and I'm just not used to it. I hope the bus comes soon. Are you studying at BFSU too?

Tim: Yeah. You too, huh? Where are you from?

Gary: Australia. And you?

Tim: The States — California. I'm Tim, by the way.

Gary: Hi, Tim. I'm Gary. There seems to be hundreds of foreign students on campus. I keep seeing new faces ...

Conversation 4

Maggie: Joyce! Hello.

Joyce: Hi, Maggie. How are you?

Maggie: I'm fine. How are you?

Joyce: Busy, as usual. I'm just looking for a birthday card for my mother. They're all so expensive!

Maggie: I know. I've just chosen this one for a friend ... and look at the price!

Joyce: Unbelievable ... Anyway, what happened to your new flat?

Maggie: Ah! That's a long story ...

Conversation 5

Doctor: Now, good afternoon ... er ... Mr. Carter. Have a seat.

Mr. Carter: Good afternoon, Doctor Chapman.

Doctor: So, what can I do for you? What seems to be the problem?

Mr. Carter: I'm not really sure but I keep getting headaches ...

Conversation 6

Mark: Hi! There's a pretty good choice of food, isn't there?

Sophie: Yeah! This salad's great. You should try some.

Mark: Thanks, I will. You didn't make it, by any chance, did you?

Sophie: No! I wish I had. I'm Sophie, by the way. Sophie Frampton.

Mark: I'm Mark Saunders. Pleased to meet you, Sophie. You don't mind me calling you Sophie, do you?

Sophie: No, of course not.

 Part 5: Track 003　　（請配合032頁及音檔使用）

Sara:

I love this photo. It's quite a good one of everyone. It really captures the moment. We were all looking so tired at the end of a long day. It was a good picnic though. Three generations together ... having fun and eating too much! Look, I'm in the middle wearing a long-sleeved, checked dress. I should have worn shorts. It was a hot day.

And that's Richard, behind me, the tall guy with the short, dark hair. He's always elegant even when he's wearing jeans and a tee shirt as he is here. He always wears a suit and tie for work, of course. He usually wears glasses but he took them off for the photo. He thinks he looks more handsome without them! The older lady, the plump one there, sitting under the tree on the left ... wearing the flowered dress ... is my mum. Isn't she great? She's always happy. This is a lovely photo of her. The person beside her is Li Ting, our Chinese neighbour ... You can't see her very well ... Her sunhat is hiding her face. She often joins us for family occasions. She really likes children and always keeps the boys entertained. She's wearing a gorgeous silk dress with tiny stars. Can you see them? They're not very clear, I'm afraid. The other woman, the one in jeans, is my friend, Val. She's great fun. She always wears casual clothes. And there's my brother, Danny — the guy in the striped shirt, looking crazy as usual. He always wears sneakers ... even for work.

Li Ting:

This is a photo of a picnic I had with my neighbours, the Black family ... or the Blacks as we call them. That's Sara Black ... That's her husband, Richard and that's Danny, her brother who has a striped shirt on. Sara's father, the older man on the right is a lovely man — very distinguished looking ... with white hair and a moustache. The children are great too. Sara has twin boys, Tom and Sam. They're identical. Can you see them? They usually wear school uniform and then it's impossible to tell them apart — both in grey trousers, white shirts and dark blue jackets — and they often play tricks on people ... but, here in the photo, they're wearing different clothes. Let me see ... Yes, that's Tom. He's wearing shorts and a striped tee shirt and Sam is in shorts and a plain tee shirt. Sam is the one in the baseball cap. The other boy, the one in sunglasses, is Tim, Val's son. Val is the woman in jeans and a checked shirt ... with short wavy hair. The young girl wearing the short skirt and spotted blouse is Helen. She has lovely, straight, blond hair. Don't look at me! It's a terrible photo of me.

 Part 6: Track 004　　（請配合041頁及音檔使用）

Mrs. Black: Did you hear the forecast, Helen? Is this awful rain going to carry on?

Helen:　　Yes, Mum. They say it will go on for at least two more days. It's really depressing, isn't it?

Mrs. Black: Yes ... and I'd love to dry all the laundry outside. I'm tired of having it hanging around in the house. Where are Tom and Sam? They should be up by now.

Helen: No way! We always have to call them a thousand times.

Mrs. Black: Well, they'll have no time for breakfast if they don't hurry up. Go and yell at them, will you?

Helen: Tom! Sam! Get out of bed ...

Mrs. Black: I said GO ... don't shout! Your father's still trying to sleep. He didn't get back till the middle of the night. (*pause*) Oh, Richard, you're already up. Sorry we disturbed you ...

Mr. Black: Oh, Sara! It's not your fault! The boys always cause trouble in the mornings, don't they? ... Anyway, I'd like something to eat and then I can go back to bed!

Mrs. Black: Right. You can have these eggs. I've done them for Tom and Sam. Anyway, your mum called yesterday. She and your dad are coming over for the weekend.

Mr. Black: This weekend? When exactly?

Mrs. Black: Well, Mary's longing to see her grandchildren as usual so she hopes to get here on Friday evening. But Henry wants to play golf on Saturday so he'll drive over on Saturday evening.

Mr. Black: Helen should be back by then, shouldn't she? She's spending Friday night with her mother.

Mrs. Black: Oh, yes, it's good you reminded me. I'd clearly forgotten ... but I never want to remember anything that concerns your dear ex-wife!

Mr. Black: Honey! Alice isn't that bad, is she? Just a bit selfish at times ... and Helen always seems to have fun with her these days.

Mrs.Black: Yes, you're right. I guess I'm still a bit jealous that she's Helen's real mother!

Mr. Black: But Helen adores you, doesn't she?

Mrs. Black: Yes, I know. And she's such an angel compared with our two boys ... Where are they?

Mr. Black: That's them now, isn't it?

Mrs. Black: Right, I'll go up and have my shower now. You keep an eye on them.

You've eaten their eggs so just give them some cereal.

Mr. Black: No, I can do some more eggs for them ...

Mrs. Black: Richard ... you spoil them. They could have had eggs if they had gotten up when I first called them ...

Mr. Black: Didn't you love to stay in bed when you were their age? And, in fact, you'd also love to stay in bed these days, wouldn't you?

Mrs. Black: Yes, OK, OK. You win ...

 總復習聽力原文：Track 005　（請配合065頁及音檔使用）

Matchmaker: Now, Mr. Li, let me explain what our agency is about. We introduce people to each other ... that is to say, men to women, and women to men ... for the sake of friendship. We cannot promise romance or marriage, but we try to match people with similar interests and attractions. The rest is, of course, up to them. Some people get on very well and others may not like each other for some reason. We have had a lot of success though, and several marriages.

David Li : Yes. I see. Well, I am really looking for a young woman I can go out with and have a good time. I am still young, so I am not desperate yet for marriage.

Matchmaker: Well, that's a good attitude to have. So, you are looking for someone around the same age as you, let's say 23—27?

David Li : Yes, that's right.

Matchmaker: Now, let's see what sort of things you expect from your ideal partner. Let's start with educational background, shall we?

David Li : Ah, well, you know, I am a university graduate myself and I would prefer my partner to be the same. So, someone with a good educational background.

Matchmaker: Mmm ... any particular subject area?

David Li : No, not really. I studied Engineering myself, but I don't necessarily want my partner to have come from the same background. Any subject area would do.

Matchmaker:	What about her profession?
David Li :	Well, again, I don't mind. I think I would rather have someone who works in the private sector than the state sector. Someone a little ambitious, maybe.
Matchmaker:	What about her personality and looks?
David Li :	Well, as you can see, I am not very tall myself, so I would prefer my partner to be shorter than me. So, under 1 meter 65.
Matchmaker:	Uh. What about her build?
David Li .	Well, preferably not too fat, but also not too thin. I don't like skinny women.
Matchmaker:	Are there any other physical features you insist on?
David Li :	Well, ... let me see ... it's not essential, but I really love long hair on women. I don't find very short hair attractive.
Matchmaker:	Okay. Now what about her personality?
David Li :	Ah yes. Well, as I said, I would like my partner to be a little ambitious ... someone lively with a good sense of humour. I don't want someone too shy, or lacking in self-confidence. But she must be kind and not too selfish or greedy.
Matchmaker:	And finally, her interests?
David Li :	Well, I like to go out a lot — I mean, I go out to restaurants, cafés, pubs ... I'm a sociable person. I love dancing, so I would like my partner to be a good dancer. I also like sport, so it would be good if she appreciated some of my sports too. For example, if she liked watching football and basketball ... you see, I play both.
Matchmaker:	What about intellectual interests, Mr. Li?
David Li :	Oh, well, I'm an outdoor person really. The only thing I do indoors is working on my computer. So, I want someone who will go out a lot with me and don't want to sit in and watch TV all the time.
Matchmaker:	I see. Well, let's look at some potential candidates, shall we?

Unit 2 家 The Home

Unit 2 家
The Home

世界上大部分人的都有一個家。家通常是我們所知道的最甜蜜、最舒服的地方。有些人一輩子都住在同一個地方，有些人則常常搬家。有些房子（house）或公寓（flat）可能同時有很多人住，但有些時候只有自己一個人住。家可能是個小小的房間（room）、宿舍（dormitory）或者是一座大城堡（castle）……

 暖身練習，重新找回用英文進行日常對話的記憶

▶ 請將下面的問題與答案配對。

What sort of place do you live in? • | • I live with my parents.

What's your flat like? • | • I live in a dormitory.

Who do you live with? • | • It's quite nice ... but ...

Tell me about your house! • | • We have our own kitchen...

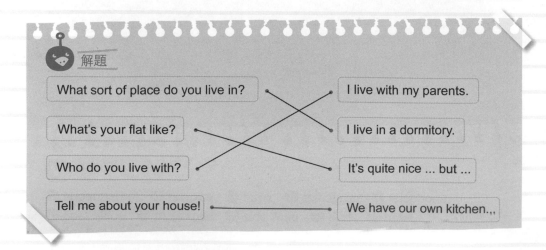

解題

What sort of place do you live in? — I live with my parents.

What's your flat like? — I live in a dormitory.

Who do you live with? — It's quite nice ... but ...

Tell me about your house! — We have our own kitchen.,,

Part 1──
10年英語不白學！
如何描述你的家

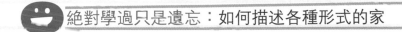 絕對學過只是遺忘：如何描述各種形式的家

前面我們提到了五種不同的家，有不同的地點或建築，都是人們可以住的地方。是哪五種呢？我已經在下面的橫線上寫出其中一種了，你可以把前面提到的其他四種都寫出來嗎？請注意我用了複數，你也應該要用複數。

Q 寫下其他四種家。

<u>houses,</u>

在上面的空白處，你應該要寫下flats（公寓），rooms（房間），castles（城堡），dormitories（宿舍）。你還知道哪些其他種類的「家」呢？有很多種，有給有錢人住的palaces（宮殿）和mansions（宅邸），還有一般人住的家。你還知道哪些其他種類的一般人的家呢？在下面的橫線上寫出來。

Q 請寫下至少三種一般人的家。

結果你寫了哪些呢？不知道你有沒有想到以下這些：

a) apartments; b) cottages; c) bungalows; d) bedsits; e) halls of residence

你可以把這五個字和下面的定義與說明配成對嗎？在每個說明旁邊寫下正確的字母。我已經填了第一題當作範例了。如果不確定單字的意思，可以查辭典！

Q 請將下面的定義和說明與上述的單字/片語配對。

① large buildings where students live in single or double rooms ___e___

② small houses in the countryside _____

③ British people use the word "flats" but Americans use this word _____

④ houses in cities which have only one storey/floor _____

⑤ single rooms which are used for cooking, eating, sleeping etc. _____

 解題

你答得如何？apartment這個詞是美式英文，而flat是英式英文！那flat/apartment到底是什麼樣子的呢？這種房子自己的大門，位於一棟大樓中，大樓裡面還有很多這樣的房子。在英式英文中，這種大樓叫做a block of flats，在美式英文中，這種大樓叫做apartment house或apartment building。英國的學生通常都住halls of residence，美國學生一般都住dormitories。你可能也沒學過bedsit這個單字。它指的是臥室兼起居室的兩用房間，在裡面可以吃飯、睡覺、工作、還能做飯。在英國較大的城鎮中都可以找到bedsits。

答案：① e; ② b; ③ a; ④ c; ⑤ d

😃 絕對學過只是遺忘：如何聊聊你的家

讓我來簡短地跟你聊聊我的家。

I like my home. I live in a flat with my parents and my sister. We have three rooms, a small hallway and our own kitchen and bathroom. I'd like to live somewhere bigger, but the flat is very comfortable. My mother does most of the household chores and my sister and I help her. I look forwards to having my own home one day.

想想看，你的家是什麼樣子？

- Is it a room, a dormitory, a flat or a house (or any of other types we have mentioned)?

- Who do you live with?

- Are you satisfied with your home or would you like to make some changes?

- Who does the household tasks/chores?

- When you decided to take part in this course, did you give some of your usual tasks to other family members so that you would have more time for study?

 請用四到五個句子，簡短說明你家目前的狀況。使用與前面短文中用到的類似的句型，盡量用到以下這些動詞：

lives/live, has/have, does/do , likes/like, would like ('d like)

　　把這些句子寫在筆記本上，大聲對自己說說看！注意以上這些動詞，確保你在使用一般現在式的時候保持主謂一致。另外 would like 後面要用動詞不定式。

　　現在更仔細地想想自己的家。如果你住在宿舍，吃、睡、工作、休息都在同一個房間，那請你想想你父母的家，甚至朋友的家（也就是說，請想像一個不只有一個房間的家）。

回答以下問題：

ⓐ How many rooms are there in addition to the kitchen and bathroom?
ⓑ Do you have your own room or do you share a room?
ⓒ What do you do there, apart from sleeping?
ⓓ Does each room in your home have a specific function or does one room serve several functions?

接下來，請你根據下面的建議和指引完成表格。

你一定還想知道更多！

　　我想你們的家除了廚房和浴室以外，還有別的房間吧？那就請你想像最重要的三個房間。如果你們家只有一個或兩個房間，那表格裡的2和3就不要填。在右欄中填入你通常在相應的房間中做的事情。舉例來說，在我家，我們都會在主要的房間（我稱為room 1）裡面吃飯，所以我就會在room 1的右欄寫下 "having meals"。請從你們吃飯的房間開始，寫下你在那個房間裡和其他房間裡還會做哪些事。注意到沒？我們都用「動詞原形+ing」來講述我們做的事。在這裡，「動詞原形+ing」是當作名詞來用的。我們可以說：

The kitchen is for food preparation.

or

The kitchen is for preparing food.

也就是說，for這個字後面要接名詞或名詞片語才行。

 請完成這個表格。寫下你家每個房間的功能或你在裡面會從事的活動。

Room	Activity
room 1	having meals
room 2	
room 3	
the kitchen	preparing meals
the bathroom	going to the toilet
the hallway	

解題

你列出了多少種活動呢？我猜你很可能列出了以下這些活動：

sleeping, dressing, washing, taking a shower/having a bath, relaxing, watching television, reading, chatting, preparing lessons, cooking, storing food, storing clothes, washing clothes, ironing, writing letters, hanging coats

絕對學過只是遺忘：建築怎麼說

　　我們討論過各種不同的家和我們在家裡都做什麼後，接下來就來談談家的建築結構本身，復習一下和建築有關的單字。

　　你能指出下面這些建築中，各個部分的英文怎麼說嗎？圖A是英國很常見的一種房子。圖B你應該覺得很眼熟吧？

　　把方框中的單字和圖片中數字指出的地方配對。在每個單字旁的橫線上寫下對應的數字。我已經替你做好第一題了！

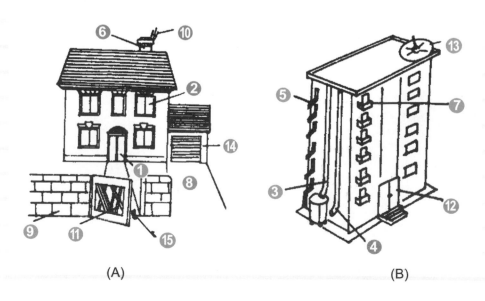

(A)　　　　　　　　　　　　　　(B)

把兩張圖中的數字寫在下面方框中對應的單字旁的橫線上。

a) balcony __7__	b) gate ___	c) window ___
d) fire-escape ___	e) garage ___	f) front door ___
g) main entrance ___	h) rubbish chute ___	i) chimney ___
j) drainage pipes ___	k) driveway/drive ___	l) TV aerial ___
m) satellite dish ___	n) path ___	o) garden wall ___

解題

上面方框中可能有幾個單字對你來說很陌生。drive或driveway就是通往garage（車庫）的私人道路，rubbish chute是英式英文，指的是一個管道，居民可以透過它把垃圾往外丟，然後垃圾就會漂漂亮亮地滑進公寓外面的大垃圾箱裡。美式英文中，則是叫garbage chute。fire escape指的是一種在室外的樓梯，出現火災等其他緊急事件的時候可以用。獨棟房子的大門叫做front door，而公寓的大門則叫entrance或main entrance。在英文中，gate（大門）指的不是大樓的大門，通常是在外牆上的一個開口。

答案：a: ⑦; b: ⑪; c: ②; d: ⑤; e: ⑭; f: ①; g: ⑫; h: ③; i: ⑥; j: ④; k: ⑧; l: ⑩;
　　　m: ⑬; n: ⑮; o: ⑨

Part 2—
10年英語不白學！
菲利普和安的新家

在這個練習中，你會聽到英國夫妻菲利普和安以及他們的三個孩子的故事。他們剛在英國的利茲買了一棟房子。這是棟兩層樓的獨棟房子，有一個院子，一個車庫，就像圖中看到的一樣。

 絕對學過只是遺忘：聊聊新房子

　　菲利普和安帶了他們的好朋友史蒂夫參觀這棟房子。史蒂夫參觀完以後回到家，跟他太太瓊描述這棟新房子。他太太問了一大堆問題。聽聽看史蒂夫如何形容這棟房子的房間配置（聽到 to give them time to get everything sorted out first 為止），回答以下問題。只需要以筆記形式在每題旁邊寫下答案就好。

🔊 聽音檔，回答以下問題。　　🔈 *Track 006*

① Where is June when Steve arrives?

② What does Steve think of the house?

③ What does Ann enjoy doing, according to June?

④ What kind of house is it?

⑤ How many rooms are there?

⑥ Why does Steve say to June that she will be seeing the house soon?

解題

答案：

1 She is in the kitchen.

2 The house is great.

3 She enjoys gardening.

4 It is a detached house with two storeys.

5 There are seven rooms.

6 Because Ann and Philip are having a house-warming party in about three weeks' time.

注意：house-warming party如字面上所見，指的是要讓新家變得「溫暖」的聚會，由新家的主人在剛搬進去時舉辦。

 絕對學過只是遺忘：**了解措辭**

　　再聽一遍對話的第一部分，寫下瓊和史蒂夫究竟用了哪些詞彙來描述以下這些事項。

🔊 聽音檔，寫下音檔中確切的用詞。 ◀ *Track 006*

ⓐ Steve is sorry that June didn't visit Ann and Philip's house with him.

He says: _____

ⓑ Steve says the garden is untidy.

He says: _____

ⓒ June says that Ann didn't like living in a small flat.

She says: _____

解題

答案：

ⓐ It's a real pity you couldn't come.

ⓑ The garden's a bit of a mess at the moment.

ⓒ Ann was fed up with living in that cramped flat.

😄 絕對學過只是遺忘：捕捉細節

回到對話最開始的地方，聽整個對話。在聽的時候，填寫以下表格左欄（暫時忽略右欄）。寫下史蒂夫提到的房間名稱。我已經替你填好一些了！

🔊 在左欄Room下面填寫史蒂夫提到的房間名稱。 🔊 *Track 006*

Room	Location
1. sitting room	downstairs, through the front door, on the right
2.	
3.	
4.	
5. downstairs bathroom	
6. cloakroom	
7.	
8.	
9.	

續表

Room	Location
10. the big storage cupboard	
11.	

 絕對學過只是遺忘：**房間的位置**

　　再聽一遍對話，把上面的表格右欄填寫完整，以描述每個房間的位置。請看看我的例子：我寫了downstairs和兩個介系詞片語through the front door和on the right。在描述其他的房間時，你也應該這樣回答，要說出房間在樓上還是樓下，然後加上史蒂夫用到的介系詞片語。如果聽不清楚，還可以再重新聽一遍音檔！

🔊 在表格右欄Location下填入每個房間的位置。 🔊*Track 006*

 解題

答案：

Room	Location
1. sitting room	**downstairs, through the front door, on the right**
2. dining room	**downstairs, on the left of the front door**
3. the kitchen	**downstairs, the second room on the left, right next to the dining room**
4. the study	**downstairs, beside the kitchen**
5. downstairs bathroom	**downstairs, on the other side of the study, on the left of that corridor**
6. cloakroom	**downstairs, next to the downstairs bathroom**
7. the big bedroom	**upstairs, the first on the left**

續表

Room	Location
8. three medium-sized bedrooms	upstairs, one next to the big storage cupboard, on the left two bedrooms on the right
9. upstairs bathroom	upstairs, next to the big bedroom
10. the big storage cupboard	upstairs, next to the upstairs bathroom
11. the small storage cupboard	upstairs, at the end of the upstairs hall

☺ 絕對學過只是遺忘：讀懂房間配置圖

　　現在請利用你在前面的表格中填好的資訊，搭配下面的房間位置圖，在以下表格中寫出各個字母處是哪個房間。也可直接把房間的名字寫在房間位置圖上，查找更便利。

GROUND FLOOR

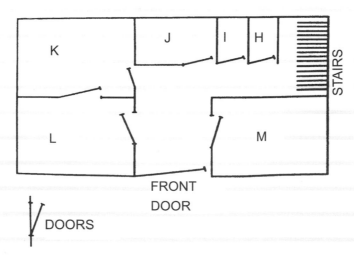

UPPER FLOOR

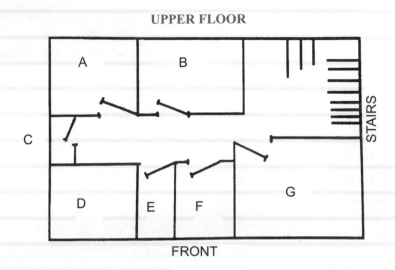

依據以上房間位置圖，把每個房間的名字寫在搭配的字母旁邊。

A	**a bedroom**	**H**	
B		**I**	
C		**J**	
D		**K**	
E		**L**	
F		**M**	
G			

解題

答案：

B. a bedroom; C. a storage cupboard; D. a bedroom;
E. a storage cupboard; F. an upstairs bathroom; G. Ann and Philip's bedroom;
H. a cloakroom; I. a bathroom; J. a study; K. a kitchen; L. a dining room;
M. a sitting room

 絕對學過只是遺忘：帶著客人參觀房子

我們想像一下，如果我們現在正在安和菲利普家幫他們接待參加喬遷聚會的客人，客人不知道每個房間在哪裡，那我們要怎麼跟他們說呢？看看以下的對話：

Philip: Hi, Julia. Come in. It's good to see you.

Julia: Hi, Philip. This is a really lovely house. Ann must be so happy.

Philip: Yes, she is. She's in the kitchen. She's dying to see you.

Julia: And I'm looking forwards to seeing Ann, so I'll go and find her. Where's the kitchen?

Philip: Go straight ahead. It's the second door on the left.

有沒有注意到？菲利普在描述廚房的位置時，說the second door on the left。如果餐廳的門是開的，朱莉亞可以直接看到餐桌和椅子，她就知道餐廳在哪裡了，那菲利普也可以說next to the dining room。他一開始是說go straight ahead，不過如果有需要左轉或右轉，他也可以說turn right或turn left。

現在，你正站在房子的大門旁邊。有些客人跑來問你以下這些問題，你該怎麼回答呢？請記得，如果你要指引客人去樓上，要說It's upstairs.。請把你會使用的描述方式寫在下頁的橫線上。

🔊 聽對話，請把你會使用的描述方式寫在下面的橫線上。 🔊 *Track 007*

ⓐ Philip said I should put my coat in his bedroom. Where is it?
You say: It's upstairs — the first door on the left.

ⓑ I hear all the drinks are in the study. But where is the study?
You say: _____

ⓒ Could you tell me where the bathroom is? I'd like to wash my hands.
You say: _____

ⓓ Do you happen to know where the cloakroom is?
You say: _____

ⓔ Ann asked me to get something from the big storage cupboard. Do you know where that is?
You say: _____

解題

選擇用哪些詞還不是唯一的問題，你還要知道怎麼說出這些詞！以上的練習及答案也有音檔，可以聽聽看，一邊對答案，一邊跟著音檔唸出來。你也可以自己做一些其他的練習，想像一下自己的學校或工作地點，想想看如何指點別人走才能找到一些房間，例如：校長辦公室、男廁、女廁等。注意指路的時候一定要講得很清楚，越簡單越好！

答案：
ⓑ Go straight ahead and turn right. It's the first door on the left.
ⓒ It's upstairs — the second door on the left.
　OR
　Go straight ahead and turn right. It's the second door on the left.
ⓓ Go straight ahead and turn right. It's the third door on the left.
ⓔ It's upstairs — the third door on your left.

Part 3——
10年英語不白學！
在家裡做的那些事情怎麼說

現在我們對菲利普與安的家已經很熟了。接下來聽一段對話，其中安在和一個華人朋友李燕描述她自己、菲利普和孩子們在家裡的房間中都做哪些事。李燕覺得有些房間的功能好像和華人家庭的不太一樣。

絕對學過只是遺忘：帶李燕參觀房子

這是一個輕鬆簡單的練習，仔細聽對話，把安帶李燕參觀的房間按照順序寫下來。

把安帶李燕參觀的房間按照順序寫下來。　◀ *Track 008*

❶ the sitting room

❷

❸

❹

❺

❻

解題

❷ dining room; ❸ the kitchen; ❹ Philip's study; ❺ the downstairs bathroom ; ❻ the cloakroom

😊 絕對學過只是遺忘：**了解大意**

　　仔細聽音檔，試著寫下安究竟講了哪些單字，引導李燕參觀房子。每題只要寫下簡短的句子即可。

Ann begins the conversation with the words:

Would you like me to show you around?

 寫下安的話。　◀Track 008

ⓐ They begin with the sitting room. What does Ann say?

ⓑ They then go to the dining room. What does she say?

ⓒ Then they arrive in the kitchen. What does she say?

ⓓ Then, what does she say to suggest that they leave the kitchen?

ⓔ What does she say when they arrive at Philip's study?

ⓕ What does she say when they arrive at the downstairs bathroom?

👽 解題

安與李燕的對話不算正式，也不算很口語，我們稱作「中庸」的風格。請記得，這個風格很實用，因為無論什麼場合幾乎都能用。也就是說，無論是參觀你家還是什麼更正式的場合，都一樣能用得上。

ⓐ Let's start with the sitting room.
ⓑ Let's move on to the dining room.
ⓒ Here we are: the kitchen!
ⓓ Shall we move on?
ⓔ This is Philip's study ...
ⓕ ... this is the downstairs loo ... or bathroom.

你可能發現，安在介紹一樓廁所時說： This is the downstairs loo ... or bathroom.這裡loo是口語化的英式英文單字，意思是「廁所」。

你可以自己練習一下，想像一下你要帶著客人參觀你的家，你會說什麼呢？仔細想想，並大聲說出來。回頭再聽聽音檔，模仿安說這些句子的方式。

😀 絕對學過只是遺忘：如何稱讚別人

李燕在參觀安的家的時候，表現出很有興趣的樣子，也說了很多讚美的話。她對以下的房間有哪些讚美呢？

 寫下李燕用了哪些單字讚美這些房間。 ◀ *Track 008*

ⓐ the sitting room: It's great — so _____.

ⓑ the dining room: It's also _____.

ⓒ the kitchen: It's a _____ kitchen.

ⓓ Philip's study: I'd _____ like this!

ⓔ the cloakroom: That must be _____!

🔬 解題

能稱讚別人總是好事，可是如果一直用一樣的單字或句子稱讚別人就會有點單調。請看看李燕所說的話，用了很多不同的形容詞。她使用了句型：it's+形容詞，反意疑問句句型：It's a lovely big kitchen, isn't it? 以及 I'd love to have a room like this.來表達自己的情感。她還用了That must ...（That must be handy.）。

ⓐ light and spacious; ⓑ very pleasant; ⓒ lovely big; ⓓ love to have a room; ⓔ handy

😃 絕對學過只是遺忘：多多使用正面的形容詞

這個對話中還出現了很多形容詞，比如：

busiest	spacious	convenient	automatic
wonderful	electric	tricky	handy

下面可以找到這些形容詞的意思和在此對話中的用法。想想每個單字的意思，並把它們填在下面的橫線上。我已經為你完成第一題了！

Ⓠ 將以上形容詞與其定義互相搭配起來。

ⓐ extremely pleasing   wonderful

ⓑ powered by electricity (i.e. not by gas)   _____

ⓒ quite difficult and inconvenient   _____

ⓓ working without needing to be operated by a person   _____

ⓔ useful/working well for the purpose it is designed   _____

ⓕ an informal word for useful   _____

ⓖ large with a feeling of space   _____

ⓗ used most often! having lots of activity   _____

解題

b electric; **c** tricky; **d** automatic; **e** convenient; **f** handy; **g** spacious; **h** busiest

絕對學過只是遺忘：使用負面形容詞

　　形容地點時，我們不會每次都用正面的形容詞。看看下面的說明，每段說明中都有個空格，請填入以下這些形容詞。我已經替你填好第一題了！

shabby, grubby, stuffy, crowded, gloomy

從上面選擇適當的形容詞填入空格中。

❶ I have only one small room. It's full of all sorts of different pieces of furniture so it's very <u>crowded</u>: I sometimes find it hard to work there. I can hardly move!

❷ I have two rooms but they each have only one small window so they are very _____. I have to have the lights on all the time.

❸ Our room is quite large but it's very old and all the furniture needs replacing. At the moment, I'm a bit ashamed of it, even though I keep it very clean. It's so _____. I'd love to paint it and buy a new bed and so on.

❹ My room is in a new building but it's quite small and the ceiling is very low. It's really _____ and I feel I want to have the windows open all the time to let some air in.

⑤ My room is lovely but it's not in a very nice building. Nobody ever cleans the staircase or hallway so they are full of rubbish and dust ... very _____, in fact.

 解題

你認識這些形容詞嗎？gloomy指的就是暗暗的、黑黑的、讓人很抑鬱的感覺。shabby是用來形容東西破破舊舊的，需要修了，但不一定是髒的。grubby指的是有一點髒髒的，但不算是很髒。stuffy指的是空氣不好的，不通風的。crowded這個字很簡單，你應該已經知道了吧！

❷ gloomy; ❸ shabby; ❹ stuffy; ❺ grubby

Part 4—
10年英語不白學！
復習一下關於家的一切

請你再聽一遍對話，仔細聽取對話中的具體資訊。  **Track 008**

😀 絕對學過只是遺忘：確認在家中的活動

看看下面表格中的活動。對話中提到一些，但有些沒有提到。聽對話，然後：

a) 把提到過的活動打勾（√），沒有提到的則打個叉（╳）。

b) 在所有提到的活動中，寫下這些活動是在哪個房間裡進行的。我已經替你舉了一些例子了！

📢 把提到過的活動打勾（√），沒有提到的則打個叉（╳）。在所有提到過的活動中，寫下這些活動是在哪個房間裡進行的。 **Track 008**

Activity	√or ╳	Room
watching TV and videos, reading, chatting		
reading, chatting to friends, listening to music, doing homework, sleeping		Children's bedroom
doing woodwork, repairs etc.	╳	
keeping the refrigerator and washing machine		
having family meals and dinner parties		
doing sewing, ironing, painting		

續表

Activity	√or ✕	Room
doing the cooking and preparing food		
working, reading, writing letters		
playing table tennis, doing physical exercise etc.		
storing books, official documents, work papers and files		
visitors washing hands, using the toilet		
hanging coats etc.		
eating breakfast		
making telephone calls		

解題

以上對話沒有提到的活動是：doing woodwork, repairs etc.（做木工、修理等）；doing sewing, ironing, painting（縫紉、燙衣服、繪畫）；playing table tennis, doing physical exercise etc.（打乒乓球、運動）；making telephone calls（打電話）。建議對照126頁的音檔原文，檢查一下你在第三欄中寫下的答案是否正確。

😃 絕對學過只是遺忘：了解菲利普和安的家

以下這段文章中描述了菲利普和安的家，先閱讀一遍，再試著利用上一題中的資訊把適當的單字填入空格中。注意：如果填不出來，可以再聽一遍音檔。需填入的單字可能是形容詞、名詞（包括-ing形式的動名詞）或動詞。

🔊 把適當的單字填入空格。　◀ *Track 008*

Philip and Ann live in a (1) _____ with their three children. They (2) _____ seven rooms as well as a kitchen, two bathrooms, a cloakroom, a hallway and storage cupboards. The (3) _____ room is the busiest room in the house. It's a room for (4) _____ . They (5) _____ TV and videos there, read and (6) _____. They usually (7) _____ breakfast in the kitchen on (8) _____ and only (9) _____ the dining room for family (10) _____ and on (11) _____ occasions. A door in the dining room (12) _____ directly into the kitchen. Like most British families, they keep their refrigerator and (13) _____ machine in the kitchen. They have an (14) _____ cooker with an oven, a grill and four burners. Philip has a study for (15) _____, (16) _____ and writing letters. Philip and Ann (17) _____ all their books in the study and (18) _____ all their official documents in the filing cabinet there. The children all have their own (19) _____ rooms upstairs where they (20) _____, (21) _____ their homework, chat to friends, (22) _____ to music and so on. Philip and Ann's bedroom is upstairs too. The main (23) _____ is upstairs but there is also a small one downstairs. There is a cloakroom in the cupboard under the stairs for (24) _____ coats and so on.

解題

(1) house; (2) have; (3) sitting; (4) relaxing; (5) watch; (6) chat;
(7) eat/have; (8) weekdays; (9) use; (10) meals; (11) special; (12) leads；
(13) washing; (14) electric; (15) working; (16) reading; (17) keep; (18) store;
(19) separate; (20) sleep; (21) do; (22) listen; (23) bathroom;
(24) hanging or storing

聽李燕和安的對話時，你有沒有發現，原來通常中國人和英國人放置冰箱的地方不太一樣？英國人都把冰箱放在哪裡呢？

Part 5——
讓你的英文能力起死回生！
復習如何描述自己的家

前面的練習中我們已經嘗試簡單地描述自己家的情況。現在可以再延伸，使用在本單元學到的單字和更具有描述性的句子。

 救回被遺忘的英文：寫出更具有描述性的句子

 首先，讀讀下面的描述，然後嘗試著在筆記本上仿寫一段吧!

I like my home. I live in a pleasant flat with my parents and sister. We have three rooms，a hallway and our own kitchen and bathroom. The first room is the main room or living room. It's for having meals, relaxing, reading, watching television and so on. It's the busiest room in the house. The second room is my parents' room. They sleep there, and store their clothes and dress there. The third room is my room. I share it with my sister. It's quite crowded because we have lots of furniture. We sleep there, keep all our possessions, listen to music and generally relax. I also do my marking and lesson preparation there. My sister does her homework there. The kitchen is mainly for cooking and storing food but the fridge is in the living room. The bathroom is for doing all the usual personal activities and for washing clothes. We store our coats and shoes in a convenient cupboard in the hallway. I'd like to live somewhere bigger, but the flat is very comfortable. I'm looking forwards to having a home of my own one day.

請注意，這段描述在說明各個房間中所做的事情時，用了兩種不同的句型。有時是這種句型：

The kitchen is mainly for cooking and storing food.

有時是這種變化了一下的句型：

We store our coats and shoes in a convenient cupboard in the hallway.

建議同時使用兩種句型，這樣寫出來的文章才會有變化、有趣。另外注意寫作時動詞的變化，記得在一般現在式的句子中，he, she, it後要用動詞第三人稱單數形式，而I, you, we, they之後則是用動詞原形。

如果你覺得對自己的描述夠滿意了，就把它抄寫到作業本上，之後就可以給老師看了。請幫它命名為這個題目（如果你描述的是你朋友的家，則用My Friend's Home這個題目）：

My Home

Part 6——
讓你的英文能力起死回生！
使用家電

　　既然我們已經練習描述家本身了，接下來就可以考慮練習描述一些現代生活中常見的生活用品。隨著生活水準的提高，幾乎每個家庭裡都會有一些家電使我們的生活變得更容易。這些家電用英文怎麼說呢？

😀 救回被遺忘的英文：這些家電的英文怎麼說

　　想想你的家中有沒有洗衣機、冰箱、熨斗或吹風機呢？這些就是electric appliances（也可以叫home appliances）。你家有多少家電呢？最近又買了哪些呢？你知道它們的英文是什麼嗎？

Ⓠ 請為下面圖片中的電器寫入相應的英文名稱。

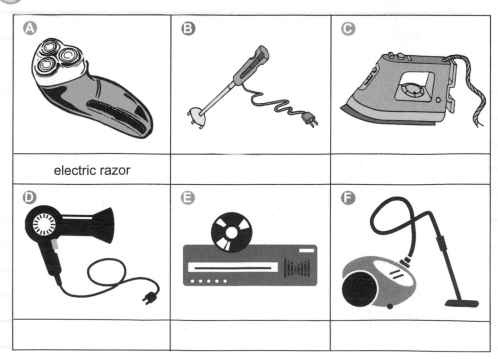

Ⓐ electric razor	Ⓑ	Ⓒ
Ⓓ	Ⓔ	Ⓕ

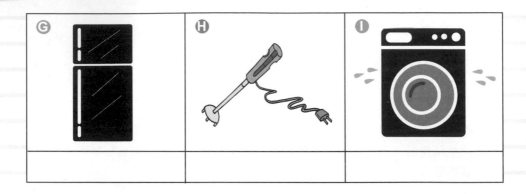

解題

B microwave oven; **C** iron; **D** hairdryer; **E** video recorder/player;
F vacuum cleaner; **G** fridge; **H** food mixer; **I** washing machine

如果你家還有其他家電，而且你不知道它們的英文名字是什麼，那就去查查看吧！家電附的使用說明書一般都會有很多種語言版本，所以你很有可能可以在上面找到它的英文名字。

救回被遺忘的英文：**如何說明家電的功能**

你可以用英文說明以上這些家電是用來做什麼的嗎？請看第一題。

Q 說明每個家電的用途。

❶ An electric razor is for shaving.

❷ A microwave oven is for _____.

③ An iron is for _____ .

④ A hairdryer is for _____ .

⑤ A video recorder is for _____ .

⑥ A vacuum cleaner is for _____ .

⑦ A fridge is for _____ .

⑧ A food mixer or blender is for _____ .

⑨ A washing machine is for _____ .

解題

② cooking food quickly

③ ironing clothes etc. (OR: removing the creases from clothes etc.)

④ drying hair quickly

⑤ recording or playing video cassettes

⑥ removing the dust from floors

⑦ storing food

⑧ mixing or blending food

⑨ washing clothes

你有沒有發現？每個句子中的for後面都用了動詞原形+ing形式。此外，每個家電前使用了a或an（而不是the），這是因為我們現在是用一個家電表示這一類別的家電。以上的句子都是很基本的「定義句」，以後還會學到更多。

你已經知道fridge這個單字了吧？其實它就是refrigerator的簡單說法，是英式英文使用者常常用的一個單字。

救回被遺忘的英文：如何讀懂使用說明書

　　電器都有個共同點：都需要用到電！我們使用電器時都必須小心謹慎，也因此會用到使用說明書。電器的使用説明書有可能很簡單，也有可能很複雜。讀讀下面簡短的説明，你能判斷這是哪種電器的使用説明嗎？

 把電器的名稱寫在對應的空格中。

Instructions for _____ Operation

First, plug the appliance into the mains socket. Then, switch it on. Use setting 1 for a normal air current and setting 2 for a strong air current. Move the appliance slowly over your hair. Do not hold it too close to the head. Do not allow it to get wet.

解題

我相信你應該很快就發現，正確答案就是Hairdryer（吹風機）。這段説明中plug和socket這兩個字很重要！英文描述中通常不需要説plug it into the socket而是用plug it in代替。連接插頭和電器的那條電線，英文叫做the flex。

 救回被遺忘的英文：了解口頭指示的正確意思

　　在基本的使用説明書中，指示通常都是用一般的動詞原形。但是口頭上的指示就不一樣了，比較複雜。
　　王文有個攪拌器，她用它來打蛋、做湯等。一天，她的一個美國朋友迪莉婭跟她借這個攪拌器，她把使用方法告訴了迪莉婭。聽音檔，看你能不能寫下王文在指示中說的五個主要的動詞（動詞原形），注意要按照順序寫！

🔊 以正確順序寫下出現在對話中的動詞。　◀ **Track 009**

❶ _____　❷ _____　❸ _____　❹ _____　❺ _____

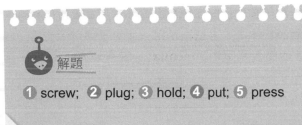

解題

❶ screw;　❷ plug;　❸ hold;　❹ put;　❺ press

😃 救回被遺忘的英文：指認電器的部位

這裡有張攪拌器的示意圖。把攪拌器各個部位的名稱寫在下圖的空白處。需要的話，可以再聽一遍音檔。

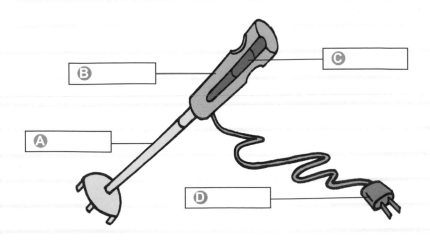

解題

Ⓐ blender arm;　Ⓑ motor body;　Ⓒ button;　Ⓓ plug

救回被遺忘的英文：練習寫使用說明書

現在你已經聽了音檔中的對話，相信你應該能寫出攪拌器的基本使用方法了吧！首先，把這些使用方法寫在筆記本上，各個指示用一個句子即可。在第一個指示前寫下first，接下來的指示前面寫下then或next。還可以加入警告用語（Don't ...）。

Ⓠ 把使用攪拌器的方法寫在筆記本上。

一旦覺得滿意了，就抄寫到作業本上，並給它命名為這個標題：

Instructions for Blender Operation

救回被遺忘的英文:比較口頭與書面的指示

再聽一遍音檔,記下王文在說明以下指示時,用到了哪些句子。

 請把音檔中聽到的相關句子寫下來。 ◀ *Track 009*

Written instruction	Spoken instruction
First, screw the blender arm into the motor body.	
Then plug it in.	Then you just plug it in.
Hold the motor body and put the blender arm into the mixture.	
Press the button.	

解題

你有沒有發現口語與書面文字的指示有點差別呢?在音檔中,你會聽到王文用這些方式開始句子:First/then/next ... you just/you have to ... 這是因為在口語中,我們一般不會直接用動詞原形下指令,而是會用you need to, you have to, you should等,這樣的句子聽起來才不會像是在命令。

答案：

Written instruction	Spoken instruction
First, screw the blender arm into the motor body.	First, you have to screw the blender arm into the motor body.
Then plug it in.	Then you just plug it in.
Hold the motor body and put the blender arm into the mixture.	Hold the motor body and put the blender arm into the mixture.
Press the button.	Then, you simply press the button ...

Part 7——
讓你的英文能力起死回生！
對付比較複雜的指示

現在我們來看看你是否能夠理解比較複雜的指示吧！

 救回被遺忘的英文：**了解特定的專有名詞**

李燕和她室友——美國女孩諾爾瑪剛買了一個蒸汽熨斗。她們還不知道怎麼用這個熨斗。你知道怎麼用嗎？李燕和諾爾瑪正在閱讀使用說明書，討論該怎麼使用。她們提到的指示中用了不少特殊的單字。要讀懂使用說明還必須認識這些單字。先閱讀下面的單字，然後聽對話。對話中提到了以下哪些物品呢？把聽到的項目打勾（√）。

把聽到的項目打勾（√）。 ◀*Track 010*

temperature knob	spray button	spray	filling hole
soleplate	water reservoir	indicator light	rear side
cord clip	measuring beaker	auto stop lamp	

解題

其實，只有以下這些單字沒有提到：
soleplate, water reservoir, cord clip, auto stop lamp

救回被遺忘的英文：學著把聽到的指示記錄下來

在進行下個練習前，先看看諾爾瑪和李燕買的這個熨斗。

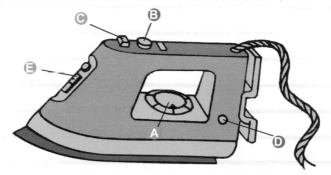

現在準備來仔細聽剛才的對話，把以下表格中每個部位的位置、形狀、大小都記錄下來。

注意：你不需要知道這些字的具體意思，只要先熟悉一下就好。

聽音檔，把聽到的以下部位的大小、形狀與位置填入下表中。 ◀ *Track 010*

Item	Size/Shape	Position
steam switch	round	on top of the handle, near the front
filling hole		
temp. knob		
indicator light		
spray button		

*表格中temp.是temperature（溫度）的縮寫。

 解題

Item	Size/Shape	Position
steam switch	round	on top of the handle, near the front
filling hole	rectangular	on the front end of the iron, below the spray
temp. knob	big, round	in the middle, under the handle
indicator light	little, round	at the back, on the handle
spray button	square	on the handle, in front of the steam switch

😀 救回被遺忘的英文：根據描述分辨出各個部位

　　請看第二題中的熨斗圖片，並根據第二大題表格中寫下的資訊認出熨斗的每個部位。

Ⓠ 在英文字母旁邊寫下熨斗每個部位的名字。

Ⓐ

Ⓑ steam switch

Ⓒ

Ⓓ

Ⓔ

🛸 解題

根據對話，我們知道steam switch是圓形的、在把手上、靠近前面。參考上面填寫的表格，我們就能判斷Ⓑ應該是steam switch。

filling hole應該是長方形的，在熨斗前端，spray的下面（Ⓔ）。

temp. knob是大大的、圓形，在把手下面中間處（Ⓐ）。

indicator light是小小的、圓形，在旁邊（Ⓓ）。

spray button是方形的，在steam switch的前面，把手上（Ⓒ）。

spray和spray button是不一樣的兩個部位！spray在filling hole的上面。

😊 救回被遺忘的英文：判斷使用熨斗的正確步驟

李燕和諾爾瑪討論了該如何使用這個熨斗。以下的步驟順序不對，請再聽一遍對話，在第一個步驟旁邊寫上1，第二個步驟旁邊寫上2……以此類推。

🔊 聽音檔，判斷哪個是第一個步驟、哪個是第二個步驟……以此類推。 🔈*Track 010*

Step		Instruction
	a	Insert the mains plug into the wall socket.
	b	Set the steam switch to the required position.
	c	Set the steam switch to position O.
	d	Set the temperature knob at the required position within the steam area.
	e	Wait a little while for the indicator light to go out.
	f	Stand the iron on its rear side and pour water into the filling hole. Use the measuring beaker for this purpose.

 解題

1. **c**; 2. **f**; 3. **d**; 4. **a**; 5. **e**; 6. **b**

救回被遺忘的英文：**如何口頭引導別人使用家電**

　　想像一下，你現在正在面對面指示別人怎麼使用熨斗。你要怎麼做呢？回想一下王文是如何教迪莉婭使用攪拌器的，她常把you放在動詞原形前面，且用了you have to/you need to等句型。現在練習一下如何教別人使用蒸汽熨斗。

Part 8——
讓你的英文能力起死回生！
請試著寫出一篇作文

這個單元已經到了尾聲了！現在就來回顧一下你在本單元學了哪些東西！

 學完這一單元，你就可以：

☐ 聊關於家的事、問關於家的問題、寫下關於家的內容

☐ 聊關於家用物品的事、問關於家用物品的問題、寫卜關於家用物品
的內容

☐ 聊或寫下關於家中不同的房間的話題

☐ 帶著別人參觀家或其他建築

☐ 給予正面評論與回應

☐ 聊或寫下家用電器的功能

☐ 讀懂、聽懂或提供使用家用電器的指示

😃 救回被遺忘的英文：練習寫出複雜但清楚的使用說明書

請你寫下一組清楚的指示，告訴他人如何使用一種家電用品，例如電鍋、吸
塵器、洗衣機等。注意使用first, next, then, finally等詞，把整組的指示寫成一段
即可。

在作業本上寫下一組指示，使用以下的標題：

Instructions for _____ Operation

總復習

 四合院

　　請聽一名記者與中式建築專家常先生的對話。常先生正在描述在中國北部（特別是北京）曾經很常見的一種傳統的四合院。

🔊 聽對話，在以下數字旁邊寫下其對應的房間名稱。 ◀ *Track 011*

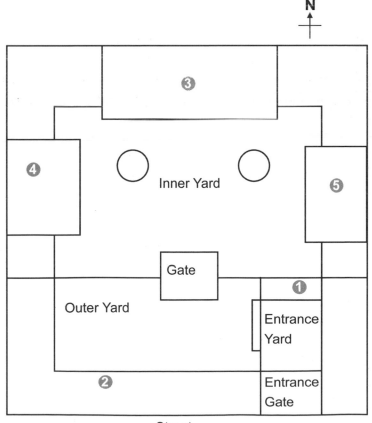

解題

1 the kitchens and storerooms

2 the servants' rooms

3 the parents' rooms

4 the rooms of their sons and their families

5 the rooms of their sons and their families

再聽一遍對話,回答以下問題。 ◀ *Track 011*

1 What does Mr. Chang mean by the "seclusion and openness" of the courtyard house?

2 Can you explain how the inner yard reflects "symmetry and balance"?

3 How did the plan of the house reflect the "hierarchy" of society at that time?

 解題

1 The family was "secluded" from the world, which meant the members were protected and lived without the noise and dirt from the street, by the walls, gates, and outer yards. Their own part of the house was very open and peaceful with a large courtyard and trees to shade it.

2 The inner courtyard is perfectly symmetrical, which means that it is the same on the right and left. If you folded a line down the middle, each side would be the same. This gives a sense of balance.

3 The rooms nearest the road were those of the lowest members of the household — the servants — then as the house became more beautiful, more peaceful and more spacious, the important members of the family lived — first the sons and their families, and at the top, the parents. That was like the hierarchy of society at the time, with the rich and powerful at the top, then their sons, then their daughters, and finally the servants at the bottom.

兩個練習都完成後，自己試著描述一個三合院或四合院的樣子吧！

MP3音檔內容完整看

若是聽完音檔還是沒把握，建議可搭配本部份學習，不熟的語彙要查辭典並作筆記，方能加深英文記憶。

 Part 2: Track 006 　　（請配合085頁及音檔使用）

Steve: Hi, June! I'm back.

June: I'm in the kitchen ... Did you go to Philip and Ann's new house?

Steve: Yes. It's a real pity you couldn't come. The house is great.

June: Come on then. Tell me all about it. I know there's a biggish garden. Ann's really excited about that. She loves flowers and gardening, apparently.

Steve: Yes ... but she'll have a lot of hard work to do first. The garden's a bit of a mess at the moment. But the house is lovely. Two storeys, detached ... and there must be ... let me see ... one, two, four, seven ... yes, seven rooms plus kitchen, bathroom and toilet.

June: Wow! That's pretty big. It must be great for them to have a house at last. I know Ann was fed up with living in that cramped flat. Do you want a coffee?

Steve: Please.

June: So, tell me all the details.

Steve: Well, you will be seeing it soon. They're having a house-warming party in about three weeks' time ... you know, to give them time to get everything sorted out first.

June: But what's it like? Give me a guided tour!

Steve: Oh, OK then. Let me see. Downstairs ... Well, you go through the front door and there's a big room on the right ... the sitting room, I suppose. They plan to put the armchairs, sofa and so on in there ... and, of course, the TV and video. On the left of the front door is the dining room. That's quite a decent size too. The second room on the left, right next to the dining room is the kitchen. There's a linking door between them. What else? Ah yes! There's also a study. It's straight ahead of you as you go in the front door ... beside the kitchen, in fact. On the other side of the study is the downstairs bathroom. I mean, there's a corridor on the right after the sitting room and the bathroom is on the left of that corridor. Then there's a cloakroom next to it ... and the stairs are at the far end.

June: It does sound big. I didn't realise there was a study downstairs. That must be great for Philip because I know he sometimes works at home. And those three teenage kids of theirs are pretty noisy at times.

Steve: Yes, Philip's delighted. He plans to have his desk and computer in there and wants to buy a filing cabinet so he can work undisturbed. The rest of the family may never see him again! I can imagine him moving his bed in there eventually.

June: Steve! Don't be ridiculous ... Anyway, what about upstairs? How many bedrooms are there?

Steve: Four, if I remember correctly. One fairly big and three medium-sized, I think. Philip and Ann are having the really nice big one at the front of the house ... It's quite separated from the other three so they'll be fairly private there!

That's first on the left ... then next to it, there's the bathroom and then another bedroom on the left as well ... and two bedrooms on the right. My only real criticism of the house is the bathroom — it's actually quite small for such a big house ... which is strange. I don't suppose it really matters but ...

June: But there's a downstairs bathroom, isn't there?

Steve: Yes, and Philip says they may be able to put a shower in there in the future. One thing I really like upstairs is the storage cupboards ... you know, those really big walk-in cupboards where you can keep all sorts of bits and pieces. There's a big one next to the upstairs bathroom. I suppose the water tank must be in there too ... and a smaller one at the end of the upstairs hall.

June: Isn't there a basement?

Steve: You know, I honestly can't remember ... I don't think so. There is a garage though, quite a big one ... so they can also store things there. Not bad, not bad at all ...

June: Sounds wonderful. I wish we could move ...

 Part 2: Track 007　　（請配合092頁及音檔使用）

a.

Guest: Philip said I should put my coat in his bedroom. Where is it?

"You": It's upstairs — the first door on the left.

b.

Guest: I hear all the drinks are in the study. But where is the study?

"You": Go straight ahead and turn right. It's the first door on the left.

c.

Guest: Could you tell me where the bathroom is? I'd like to wash my hands.

"You": It's upstairs — the second door on the left.

OR

Go straight ahead and turn right. It's the second door on the left.

d.

Guest: Do you happen to know where the cloakroom is?

"You": Go straight ahead and turn right. It's the third door on the left.

e.

Guest: Ann asked me to get something from the big storage cupboard. Do you know where that is?

"You": It's upstairs — the third door on your left.

 Part 3 & 4: Track 008   （請配合093，099頁及音檔使用）

Ann: So, would you like me to show you around?

Li Yan: Yes, please!

Ann: Let's start with the sitting room. This will almost certainly be the busiest room in the house. It's basically a room for relaxing. We watch TV and videos in here, read, chat and so on.

Li Yan: It's great — so light and spacious. Doesn't anyone sleep in here?

Ann: No, we all sleep upstairs. But the sofa is in fact a bed-settee ... I mean it does convert into a bed, so if we're short of space when people come to stay, they can sleep in here.

Li Yan: So, the children have their own separate rooms?

Ann: Yes! You can see them in a moment. You know, because they're teenagers now, they like their privacy. So as well as sleeping in their bedrooms, they do their homework, chat to friends, listen to music and so on.

Li Yan: That's lucky for them.

Ann: Yes, it is. Now, let's move on to the dining room. Here we are. This is it.

Li Yan: It's also very pleasant. And do you eat all your meals in here?

Ann: Not all meals. We usually have breakfast in the kitchen on weekdays ... and we really only use the dining room for family meals when everyone is here ... and for special occasions and dinner parties. It's quite convenient. You see, this door leads directly into the kitchen. Here we are: the kitchen!

Li Yan: Ummm! It's a lovely big kitchen, isn't it? Like something from a magazine! Do all British families keep their refrigerators in the kitchen?

Ann: Yes ... where else could they put them?

Li Yan: Well, it may seem strange to you, but in China, we don't always have the fridge in the kitchen. In my parents' house the fridge is in the main room ... the room you'd call the living room.

Ann: I see ... I suppose it's most useful in here because this is where we do the cooking.

Li Van: And is that a washing machine?

Ann: Yes, a washing machine ... so I can do the washing while I'm busy cooking or whatever in here ... because it's fully automatic.

Li Yan: An automatic washing machine makes life easy.

Ann: Yes, it does. You can imagine how much washing there is in this family! And this is my wonderful new electric cooker — I love it! It's so clean and easy to use. I always used gas before. Some people prefer gas but I like electric ...

Li Yan: I think it's great the cookers — or stoves — always have four burners in England, as well as an oven and a grill. We usually only have two burners in China ... which can be really tricky if you're trying to prepare a special meal with lots of dishes.

Ann: Umm! I can imagine. I don't think I could manage with just two burners. Shall we move on? This is Philip's study — where he works, reads, writes letters and so on. We keep all our books here on those bookshelves ... and store our official documents, important papers and so on in the filing cabinet ... and all Philip's work papers and files are in his desk.

Li Yan: Oh! I'd love to have a room like this! Do most homes have a study?

Ann: No, not really. It's quite a luxury. And, this is the downstairs loo ... or bathroom. It saves us having to go all the way upstairs to use the bathroom! And, of course, visitors tend to use this one. There's only the toilet and a hand basin in there now but Philip wants to put in a shower. And that cupboard under the stairs is a cloakroom for hanging coats and so on.

Li Yan: That must be handy!

Ann: Yes. It keeps them out of sight! I'm about ready for a cup of tea. We can look upstairs later. How about you?

Li Yan: Oh, yes, please.

Ann: Come on then. Let's go back to the kitchen.

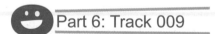 Part 6: Track 009　　（請配合109頁及音檔使用）

Delia: Can I borrow your blender? Just for tonight? I'll bring it back tomorrow.

Wang Wen: Yes, of course you can. Here it is.

Delia: Is there an instruction booklet?

Wang Wen: No, I think I've lost it. But it's very easy. You just plug it in and press the button.

Delia: It certainly sounds easy. But how do you wash it? I'm sure the motor shouldn't be put into water ...

Wang Wen: Right ... You've just reminded me. You mustn't get the motor body wet. You see the blender is actually in two parts — the motor body and the blender arm. Let's start again. It is easy to use but, first, you have to screw the blender arm into the motor body. Then you just plug it in ... Hold the motor body and put the blender arm into the mixture. Then, you simply press the button and it starts to work. As I said, it's easy.

Delia: Great ... That soup you made at the weekend was fantastic.

 Part 7: Track 010   （請配合114頁及音檔使用）

Norma: Now, let's sit down and see how it works. I'm sure it's quite easy.

Li Yan: Yes ... but let's read the manual together.

Norma: It's really not difficult. Look, it says "first set the steam switch to position O". So, which is the steam switch?

Li Yan: Let me see ... steam switch ... letter B. Look, it's this round one on top of the handle, near the front. So we should first set this to O, you say? Right. What next?

Norma: Next stand the iron on its rear side and pour water into the filling hole.

Li Yan: Now, where's the filling hole? Filling hole ... letter E. Yes, it's this rectangular hole on the front end of the iron ... below the spray, here , which is letter F ... This must be the bit that sprays water while you iron ...

Norma: Yes, I see. But which is the spray button? Here, it's this one, on the handle, in front of the steam switch ... this square one.

Li Yan: Let's go back to filling it ... How do we know how much water to put in?

Norma: It says we should use the measuring beaker.

Li Yan: Sorry, what's the measuring beaker?

Norma: It's this ... this plastic cup with a spout. There's a line on it, here, and the word "MAX" — that shows you the maximum amount of water you can put in.

Li Yan: OK, thanks. Now, where were we? What do we do after filling it?

Norma: ... Set the temperature knob ... at the required position within the steam area, it says ...

Li Yan: Umm ... I don't really follow you. Where's the temperature knob?

Norma: Here, it's this big round one, in the middle, under the handle.

Li Yan: Yes, but what do we do with it?

Norma: We turn it to the required position ... to how hot you want the iron to be.

Li Yan: And then?

Norma: Plug it in, I suppose.

Li Yan: And then start ironing?

Norma: Not immediately, no. It says you have to wait until the indicator light goes out, and then comes on again.

Li Yan: The indicator light? Ah, yes. It's this little round one, at the back, on the handle. But why do we have to wait for it to go out and then back on, I wonder?

Norma: I have no idea, but it doesn't matter. We'll just do as it says! The last step before starting to iron is to set the steam switch to the required position ... We can choose: extra steam or just steam ... you see?

Li Yan: Yes ... this is the steam switch here. We looked at it before ... here on the handle.

Norma: So, I think we can get down to work now and iron all those creased clothes.

Li Yan: Right ... I'll go and fill the measuring ... What did you call it?

Norma: Measuring beaker ...

Li Yan: OK ... the measuring beaker. I'll be back in a moment!

總復習聽力原文：Track 011　（請配合121頁及音檔使用）

Journalist: So, Mr. Chang, what we are about to enter is one of the traditional courtyard houses of Beijing, isn't it?

Mr. Chang: That's right. There are few of them existing in such a good state. This one has been preserved in the state it was originally built.

Journalist: This seems like quite a simple gate.

Mr. Chang: Yes, this is the gate people would enter from the street. You'll notice that the whole construction is facing south to benefit from the sun. As we enter, you'll see a small entrance yard.

Journalist: This is also much smaller than I thought.

Mr. Chang: Ah, well, now you will begin to appreciate the two typical features of such courtyard houses: openness and seclusion. The first part which we are experiencing now is the seclusion — that means that the very simple gate and entrance hall hide the size of the dwelling within. You see, the family is hidden and protected.

Journalist: So, these buildings here are not the family rooms?

Mr. Chang: Oh no. On the right you will see the kitchens and storerooms. This was probably always the busiest part of the house. Servants would be rushing around and delivery men would be entering from the street. So it would be busy and noisy.

Journalist: And this is another gateway on the left.

Mr. Chang: Yes. Now let's step through and enter the outer yard.

Journalist: This is certainly a little quieter, but you can still hear the noises from the street. So, what are these rooms here?

Mr. Chang: These are the servants' rooms. It's true they are close to the street and can hear all the noise out there. They are also close to the kitchens of course.

Journalist:	Now we have another gate, which is much bigger and more decorated than the first one.
Mr. Chang:	Ah, now this is the entrance to the family dwelling area. Let's go through and you can see the difference.
Journalist:	Oh, but it's lovely here. It's quiet and very peaceful. Those two trees really shade the courtyard.
Mr. Chang:	Now, what do you notice about the trees and the buildings here?
Journalist:	Well, there is a symmetry — the left side is the same as the right side.
Mr. Chang:	That's right. Symmetry and balance are also features of these traditional houses. Remember I told you that they were based on openness and seclusion. So, you see, the family was secluded in the peace and quietness of the courtyard, with walls and gates for protection around the outside.
Journalist:	Oh, yes, I can see that. This courtyard is very big too, so they had plenty of space.
Mr. Chang:	Yes, that's the openness. In fact usually up to 40 percent of the area was made up of courtyard and walkways. There are walkways going right round the courtyard, so if the weather was bad, they wouldn't have to walk in the open. You'll see that the rooms are actually quite small inside.
Journalist:	Yes, indeed. Well, who would live in the big rooms at the back of the yard, behind the trees?
Mr. Chang:	That would be the most senior members of the family — the parents. Their rooms face directly south, so they get the best of the sun.
Journalist:	And what about the rooms on the side?
Mr. Chang:	Well, on both sides, both east and west, would be the houses of the sons and their families. You see, a woman would marry into the family, so daughters always went to live with their husbands' families.

Journalist: Ah, I see. So, the whole structure of the house reflects the hierarchy of the family — the least important people live in the front of the house, and then as we go in towards the back of the house ... I suppose you could say the heart of the house ... the rooms are occupied by more and more important members.

Mr. Chang: Yes, that's it exactly. It's really an echo on a smaller scale of the imperial palaces.

Unit 3 日常事務 Daily Routines

Unit 3 日常事務

Daily Routines

我們大部分人都有一些每天要做而且比較有規律的事情。這些天天要做的事可能會花費不少時間，例如做家務、購物以及打理自己之類的事務等。有些人覺得這些事情很無聊，有些人則很享受。但無論你喜不喜歡，這些事總是得做的。不同的文化中，每天的生活規律也不太一樣。在這個單元中，你將會學到如何描述自己每天的生活習慣，以及了解英美等英語國家的人們的生活習慣。

 來個小暖身

閱讀以下的敘述，判斷哪些是表示「每天有規律地要做的事情」，哪些是表示「對於這些事情的感受」。如果是前者，請在旁邊寫下（R），如果是後者，則寫下（F）。

▶ 在以下的敘述旁邊寫下（R）或（F）。

❶ My mother does my washing for me.

❷ I enjoy housework.

❸ I often oversleep.

❹ We always have a quick breakfast.

❺ I cook twice a day.

❻ I can't stand ironing.

❼ I don't mind shopping.

解題

以上有四個敘述描述的是「每天有規律地要做的事情」，而另外三個則描述「對有些事情的感受」：I enjoy housework. I can't stand ironing. I don't mind shopping.

答案：
①R; ②F; ③R; ④R; ⑤R; ⑥F; ⑦F

Part 1——
10年英語不白學！
如何描述日常生活習慣

 絕對學過只是遺忘：每天的生活習慣

看看下面的表格，是不是列出了一些不一樣的事務呢？想像一下你人生中普通的一天或一周，看看第一欄中寫到的各種事務。然後：

a) 如果你在普通的一天或一周中會做到這件事，就在第二欄中打個勾（√）。如果你幾乎不做這件事，則打個叉（X）。

b) 對於打勾的事項，在第三欄中要寫下你做這件事的頻率。可以使用以下類似的說法：once a day（一天一次），twice a day（一天兩次），several times a day（一天好幾次），every week（每周一次），twice a week（一周兩次），three or four times a week（一周三或四次）。

c) 在第四欄中，寫下你對這些事務的感受。使用以下的符號：如果喜歡這項事務，就給它一個「+」，不喜歡則給它一個「-」。如果你覺得沒什麼特別感受，就寫下「+/-」。

我以自己為例，替你完成了這表格的一部分。從這個表格中，你可以看出：我每天都要早起，但我並不特別討厭或喜歡這件事。我不刮鬍子，每天煮兩餐，並樂在其中。我一周熨燙兩次衣服，為家具清一次灰塵，但我不怎麼喜歡做這些事。

Q 完成這個表格吧！

(1) Activity	(2) √ / X	(3) Frequency	(4) +, -, +/-
get up early	√	every day	+/-
make my bed/make the beds			
have a bath/shower			
do my hair			
put on my make-up			
shave	X		
dress/change my clothes			
cook (1,2,3 ?) meal(s)	√	every day	+
eat (1,2,3 ?) meal(s)			
wash the dishes			
shop for groceries and so on			
do the washing			
do the ironing	√	twice a week	-
dust the furniture	√	once a week	-
clean the floors			
read a newspaper			
listen to the radio/watch TV			

😃 絕對學過只是遺忘：**說說你每天的生活習慣**

根據我在表格中填的內容，我就可以說出以下這些句子來描述我自己：

I get up early every day. I don't mind getting up early.

Or: I don't particularly like getting up early but I don't dislike it either.

I cook two meals every day. I like cooking.

I dust the furniture once a week. I don't like dusting.

I do the ironing twice a week. I can't stand ironing.

注意表示「頻率」的片語（every day，once a week等），都放在句子的最後面。不過，單一的副詞（如always，never等）通常都是放在動詞的前面。如：I never shave.

表示喜歡和不喜歡的事的時候，會用以下這些用法：

(1) 喜歡的事情：like + *v.*-ing

(2) 不喜歡也不討厭的事情：

I don't mind *v.*-ing, or I don't particularly like *v.*-ing, but I don't dislike it either.

(3) 不喜歡的事情：I don't like *v.*-ing, or I can't stand *v.*-ing.

「can't stand *v.*-ing （受不了做某事）」的語氣很強烈，只有在不正式的場合而且真的很討厭某事的時候，才會這樣說。

這些句子也有音檔，你可以邊聽邊跟著讀，把這些用法牢記在心。

🔊 聽音檔，跟著讀這些句子。 🔈*Track 012*

現在就使用你剛學到的這些用法來描述自己吧！對於表格上的各項事務，都請你講一到兩句。

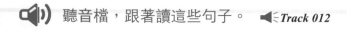

Q 練習說說自己對這些事務的感受。

😃 **絕對學過只是遺忘：如何根據日常生活習慣去了解一個人**

　　相信你應該可以從一個人天天要做的日常事務中看出他/她是個什麼樣的人吧！我們請了一個最近到北京的訪客回答了一些問題，並以他/她的回答做了一個表格（如下表）。你能從這個表格中看出這個人是怎樣的人嗎？請根據表格做以下的練習。

Activity	√ / X	Frequency	+, -, +/-
get up early	X		
make my bed/make the beds	X		
have a bath/shower	√	twice a day	+
do my hair	√	several times a day	+
put on my make-up	√	twice a day	+
shave	X		
dress/change my clothes	√	twice a day	+
cook (1,2,3 ?) meal(s)	X		
eat (1,2,3 ?) meal(s)	√	every day	+/-
wash the dishes	X		
shop for groceries	X		
do the washing	X		

續表

Activity	√ / X	Frequency	+, -, +/-
do the ironing	X		
dust the furniture	X		
clean the floors	X		
read a newspaper	√	every day	+
listen to the radio/watch TV	√	every day	+

你猜得到這個人是什麼性別、年齡、個性嗎？他/她和誰同住呢？在下面勾選出最可能的選項。你可以想想：為什麼你會覺得這個答案最有可能呢？（不過可以不必寫下原因。）

 勾出最可能的選項。

SEX: male
        female

AGE: 16 – 20
       21 – 40
       41 – 60
       61 – 90

LIVING
SITUATION:
    with husband/wife
    in a dormitory
    alone in a flat/house
    with parents

CHARACTER:
    hard-working
    lazy
    domesticated
    undomesticated
    selfish
    thoughtful

Q 現在把這些句子補充完整吧！

(sex) I imagine this person is _____;

(age) I should think _____;

(living situation) _____ probably lives _____;

(character) _____ seems to be rather _____, _____ and
_____.

Q 你覺得以下這些敘述是正確的還是錯誤的呢？正確的請圈起T
（TRUE），不正確的請圈起F（FALSE）。

❶ He/She likes sleeping.   T   F

❷ He/She likes housework.   T   F

❸ He/She pays a lot of attention to his/her appearance.   T   F

❹ He/She spends a lot of time watching TV.   T   F

❺ He/She has a lot of free time.   T   F

❻ He/She does everything for himself/herself.   T   F

❼ He/She is probably a good cook.   T   F

❽ He/She likes to know what's happening in the world.   T   F

 解題

你從這個表格得到什麼結論呢？大部分的人應該都會寫下：I imagine this person is female（我覺得這個人是女性。）；I should think she is between 16 and 20 years old（我覺得她應該是16–20歲。）；She probably lives with her parents（她應該是和父母同住。）；She seems to be rather lazy, undomesticated and selfish.（她似乎很懶惰、不愛做家務、而且自私。）

大部分的人都會認為第 ❶、❸、❹、❺、❽ 項是正確的，第 ❷、❻、❼ 項是不正確的。你覺得呢？

☺ 絕對學過只是遺忘：能不能根據日常生活習慣正確地了解一個人

這個女孩真的是這樣的人嗎？有時候以一個人的日常生活習慣來判斷她的性格，不一定是對的。這個女孩（她的名字是崔西）寫下了幾句話描寫自己的生活，我們一起來看看，或許對她的印象會有改觀。

I am studying for my 'A' level examinations so I have to study very hard these days and I never have a spare moment. I prefer to work at night when my younger brother and sisters are sleeping. I sometimes study until two or three o'clock in the morning so I get up quite late in the mornings. I listen to the radio while I'm working but I never watch television. I read the newspaper every morning while I eat breakfast — just to keep up with world events. My mother is fantastic. She never expects me to help her with the housework and happily does all my washing and ironing for me so that I have more time for my studies. I actually enjoy cooking and I don't mind housework. I just don't have time for domestic work at the moment. I get very bored with my studies at times so I often have a shower to wake me up! I always try to dress well and look good while I'm studying so I make sure my hair and make-up are OK. I think it's important to look good. There's no point in feeling miserable and looking terrible! My life won't always be like this, I'm happy to say.

Q 現在再寫下幾句話來描述崔西吧！試用下面這個句型，來表達你對她的印象是如何改觀的。

I thought Tracy was lazy but, in fact, she's hard-working.

1 (housework)

_____

2 (television)

_____

3 (free time)

_____

不過，你對她的第一印象也不見得全錯吧！例如，你可能會想說：

I thought Tracy paid a lot of attention to appearance and I was right!

解題

❶ I thought Tracy disliked housework but, in fact, she doesn't mind it.

❷ I thought Tracy watched television but, in fact, she never watches it.

❸ I thought Tracy had lots of free time but, in fact, she never has a spare moment.

腦力激盪

　　再多想幾個句子,使用類似的句型。你不一定要把它們寫下來,但有練習才會記得更牢,所以至少也要把句子多念幾次!

_____

_____

_____

　　你覺得崔西的父母會不會太寵她了呢?這也很難說,當初訪問她的時候,我並沒有感覺她很驕縱。

146 |

Part 2——
10年英語不白學！
如何用英文詢問日常生活習慣

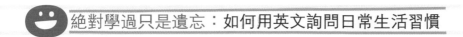 絕對學過只是遺忘：如何用英文詢問日常生活習慣

為了得到前面（P141-P142）方框中的資訊，我們問了崔西很多問題。根據下面崔西的回答，反推回來想像一下，我們問了她哪些問題呢？

Ⓠ 為以下答案寫下適當的問題。

❶ Question: _____
No, never. It's usually after eight when I get up.

❷ Question: _____
No, I don't. My mum makes the beds for the whole family.

❸ Question: _____
Twice a day, usually, if there's enough hot water.

❹ Question: _____
Three, I suppose: breakfast, lunch and dinner.

❺ Question: _____
None. My parents do all the cooking.

❻ Question: _____
No. My mum does all the household shopping. I occasionally help her.

7 Question: _____

Yes, I do actually. I like buying books, clothes and so on.

8 Question: _____

I don't mind it but I prefer listening to the radio.

9 Question: _____

Several times a day. I have very untidy hair so it always looks a mess.

10 Question: _____

No, my mum does that too. But she has an automatic washing machine so it's quite easy.

11 Question: _____

Every day. I usually read *The Times* while I'm having breakfast.

解題

問題可能有很多種不同的問法，以下只列出供參考的答案！

1 : Do you get up early?

2 : Do you make your own bed?

3 : How often do you have a bath?

4 : How many meals do you eat each day?

5 : How many meals do you cook each day?

6 : Do you ever shop for groceries?

7 : Do you like shopping? OR: Do you enjoy shopping?

8 : Do you like watching TV?

⑨ : How often do you do your hair?

⑩ : Do you do your own washing? OR: Do you wash your own clothes?

⑪ : How often do you read a newspaper?

我們來看看這些問題中使用的句型

第①、②、⑥、⑦、⑩題的答案都是yes或no，所以可以想像，問題的開頭應該是：Do you...?

第③、⑨、⑪題的答案都牽涉到做某件事情的頻率（twice a day, several times a day, every day），所以我們可以想像，問題的開頭應該是：How often...?

第④、⑤題的答案都是數字（three, none），所以我們可以想像，問題的開頭應該是：How many...?

第⑧題的答案是I don't mind it（我不介意）...，所以我們可以想像題目應該是問崔西喜不喜歡某件事務。也許題目是：Do you like...?或是：How do you feel about ...?

關於詢問日常事務的問題總結：

Yes/No questions:	Do you ...?
Questions about frequency:	How often ...?
Questions about number:	How many ...?
Questions about likes/dislikes:	Do you like ...?
OR：	How do you feel about ...?

絕對學過只是遺忘：如何用own和ever描述日常生活習慣

 閱讀以下的問題，想想看own這個字是怎麼使用的呢？

Do you make your own bed?
Do you do your own washing?/Do you wash your own clothes?

　　你知道我們為什麼會在這些問題裡面用到own這個詞嗎？因為在問這些問題的時候，我們覺得也許會有其他人幫忙做這件事。舉例來說，我們問：Do you do your own washing?（你是自己洗自己的衣服嗎？）的時候，真正想問的是：Do you do your own washing or does someone else do it for you?（你是自己洗自己的衣服，還是別人會幫你洗呢？）

　　再舉個例子，如果我們問一位男士：Do you do your own ironing?（你自己的衣服自己燙嗎？），就可以想像我們其實是想知道，他的衣服是自己燙，還是家人幫他燙。

　　接下來，看看下面這個問題中ever是怎麼用的？
Do you ever shop for groceries?

　　原來，我們在問一件我們覺得不太可能發生的事情的時候，就會用到ever這個詞。也就是說，如果我們覺得對方有可能會回答never，就可能在問句裡用到ever。除此之外，其實是不太需要用到ever的。

　　想想看，在以下的情境中，你可能會問到哪些問題呢？試試看在所提問題中使用ever或者own。

Q 寫下在以下情境中可能問到的問題。

a You see Brad, an American student who is a friend of yours. He's not very domesticated but his clothes are always very well ironed.

_____

b You're walking past some tennis courts with a friend who loves sport but you have never seen him with a tennis racquet.

_____

c It's the middle of winter and you see your friend, as usual, without a coat on.

_____

d You would like to know whether the foreign teacher you know cooks for herself or eats in restaurants.

_____

e You are impressed by your friend's complicated hairstyles. Her hair is always perfect but you know she can't afford to go to a hairdresser.

_____

f It's 10 o'clock in the morning and you meet a friend who looks as if he has just got out of bed. You realise you have never seen him early in the morning.

_____

解題

在看解答之前，先提醒一下：這些情境都是非正式的，而且說話者彼此很熟悉。因此這些問題通常都是比較私人的，不太會用來問陌生人。

a Do you iron your own clothes? OR: Do you do your own ironing?

b Do you ever play tennis?

c Do you ever wear a coat?

d Do you cook your own meals?   OR: Do you prepare your own food?

e Do you do your own hair?

f Do you ever get up early?

Part 3——
10年英語不白學！
看看布萊克家族的日常生活習慣

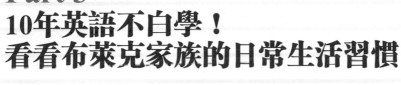 絕對學過只是遺忘：如何將布萊克家族的生活習慣整理出來

你還記得第一個單元中的莎拉・布萊克一家人嗎？在音檔中，你將會聽到他們家中的三個成員在描述自己每天早上要做的事。最先講話的是爸爸理查德，然後是媽媽莎拉，最後是兒子山姆。

聽完音檔後，判斷以下這些敘述哪些符合這三個人對「早上」的看法。替每個人選出最適當的一條敘述，並將其名字寫在橫線上。其他的橫線上打叉（╳）。

🔊 聽音檔，判斷以下敘述哪個最適合理查德，莎拉與山姆。
🔊 *Track 013*

ⓐ Morning is my favourite time of day.　＿＿＿＿＿＿＿

ⓑ I don't like mornings.　＿＿＿＿＿＿＿

ⓒ I don't like getting out of bed.　＿＿＿＿＿＿＿

ⓓ I love getting up early to take a bath.　＿＿＿＿＿＿＿

ⓔ I like to start the day slowly.　＿＿＿＿＿＿＿

ⓕ I like a quick start to the day.　＿＿＿＿＿＿＿

解題

Richard: I don't like mornings. **b**
Sara: I like to start the day slowly. **e**
Sam: I don't like getting out of bed. **c**

😊 絕對學過只是遺忘：如何辨認日常生活中的習慣

再聽一次音檔，將其中提到的事都打勾（√）。這些事是誰做的呢？請在旁邊寫下他/她的名字。

🔊 聽音檔，打勾並寫下做每件事的人是誰。 🔈 *Track 013*

1 having a quick wash   √   Richard

2 taking a bath

3 taking a shower

4 doing some exercise

5 brushing his/her teeth

6 fixing his/her hair

7 dressing quickly

8 cooking breakfast

9 ironing his/her clothes

10 making the beds

解題

除了第 ⑤ 與 ⑨ 項沒有提到，其他的選項都要打勾。

❷ Richard; ❸ Sara and Helen; ❹ Sara; ❻ Sara; ❼ Sam; ❽ Sara;
❿ Sara

 絕對學過只是遺忘：如何運用頻率副詞描述生活習慣

　　再聽一次音檔，注意「頻率副詞」（adverbs of frequency）的使用。所謂頻率副詞指的就是always（總是），sometimes（有時），usually（通常）等。將副詞寫在每一句旁邊的橫線上，並用「^」標出它在句中的位置。第一題已經為你做好示範了！

🔊 聽音檔，寫下句中的頻率副詞並標出其位置。　◀ *Track 013*

❶ Richard ^ takes a bath at night.   _usually_

❷ Richard has to drag the boys out of bed.   _____

❸ Sara gets up early.   _____

❹ Helen helps Sara prepare breakfast.   _____

❺ Helen and Sara have a quiet chat.   _____

❻ They all manage to sit down to have breakfast together.   _____

❼ Sara does ten minutes' exercise.   _____

❽ The boys take no notice of the morning call.   _____

❾ Sara looks mad at the boys because they have no time for breakfast.   _____

❿ The school bus waits for the boys.   _____

解題

② Occasionally, Richard has to ...;

③ Sara always gets up ...;

④ Helen sometimes helps ...;

⑤ Helen and Sara usually have ...;

⑥ They rarely all manage ...;

⑦ Sara always does ...;

⑧ The boys usually take ...;

⑨ Sara often looks mad ...;

⑩ The school bus always waits for ...

注意到這些頻率副詞的位置了嗎？在第2句中，位置比較不一樣對不對？在其他句中，副詞都是放在主語與動詞中間，而第2句中，副詞則是放在最開頭的地方。其實，這是因為在非正式用語中，有時候也可以用頻率副詞來做句子的開頭，或把頻率副詞放在句子的最後面（如：We get up late sometimes.）。但最安全的做法還是培養把頻率副詞放在主語與動詞中間的好習慣。

我們來看看這些頻率副詞所表示的頻率程度。

usually, occasionally, always, sometimes, rarely, often, never

always是用來說「總是」在發生的事，never則是「從來不」發生的事。其他的頻率副詞呢？

Q 完成這個表格。

most often	always
	occasionally
never	never

解題

正確的順序應該是：
always; usually; often; sometimes; occasionally; rarely; never

😀 **絕對學過只是遺忘：利用原因來補充描述生活習慣**

　　你可以使用because ...句型補充完整以下這些句子嗎？注意不能完全按照音檔原文直接寫下來，因為句型不完全一樣。要記得注意動詞的使用，有的應該使用第三人稱單數，有的則應該是動詞原形。

舉例來說：

理查德在音檔中說：I always take a bath at night to save time in the mornings.

我們則要把它改成：He always takes a bath at night because *he likes/ needs/wants to save time in the mornings.*

🔊 聽音檔，為以下句子填上原因。 ◀Track 013

❶ Richard has to shave in the mornings because <u>he's quite dark and hairy.</u>

❷ Sara always gets up early because _____

❸ The boys sometimes don't have time to eat breakfast because _____

❹ The boys never go to sleep until late because _____

❺ Sara is often angry with the boys because _____

❻ The boys fight in the bathroom because _____

🛸 解題

❷ ... she doesn't like to rush in the mornings.

❸ ... they get up too late/so late.

❹ ... they (always) talk in bed at night.

❺ ... they have no time to eat breakfast.

❻ ... they both need to use it at the same time.

Part 4——
10年英語不白學！
關於每個人、每種文化的飲食習慣

食物是我們日常生活中很重要的一部分！每個人、每種文化的飲食習慣都不太相同。有些人每天都正常吃三餐，有些人則只吃點心或只吃一次大餐。在某些文化中，午餐是一天中最重要的一餐，而在某些文化中晚餐又是最重要的。

😀 絕對學過只是遺忘：如何辨認不同的「餐點」名

人們吃飯的時間各有不同，不同的「餐點」名稱也不同。讀讀下面的敘述，看看這些人的飲食習慣有什麼不一樣吧！把文中提到的所有「餐點」名都畫上底線。我已經為你畫好第一個當示範了！

ⓠ 將所有「餐點」名畫上底線。

❶ Monica is a secretary in New York. She shares an apartment with two friends.

"I have a quick <u>breakfast</u> at home and a light lunch in the office at twelve thirty so I'm always very hungry in the evenings. I often eat supper at home with my roommates but we sometimes go to a restaurant. It's usually quite late, about 8:30 or 9, by the time we eat."

❷ Fred, a businessman, lives with his wife and three children in Canada.

"I eat breakfast at home before I leave for work and usually have lunch in a restaurant with clients or colleagues at around one o'clock. I always try to have supper at home with my wife and children to make sure we spend some time together in the evenings."

❸ Mrs. Lockey is a retired factory worker in England. She lives alone.

"I usually have breakfast around half past eight and dinner at about one. Tea-time is around half past five for me. I often invite friends for tea. I have a light supper, usually just a hot drink and a sandwich, at about ten o'clock."

❹ David, 22, works in a bank. He lives with his parents in London.

"I never have time for breakfast in the mornings so I look forwards to lunchtime and usually go to a restaurant with friends from work. My lunch break is from one o'clock till two. My mother cooks dinner for the whole family in the evenings so I tend to eat at home. That's at around seven o'clock. I occasionally go out for dinner with friends. I don't bother with supper at bedtime."

❺ Jake is an Australian student who lives in a house with some friends.

"I don't have fixed meal time! I just eat when I'm hungry. I sometimes go back to my mum's house for dinner in the evenings or for brunch at weekends. She serves brunch at about eleven and that's just perfect for me because I like to stay in bed quite late on Saturday and Sunday."

 解題

❶ breakfast, lunch, supper
❷ breakfast, lunch, supper
❸ breakfast, dinner, tea, supper
❹ breakfast, lunch, dinner, supper
❺ dinner, brunch

想要更了解這些單字的用法，就繼續做後面的練習吧！

 絕對學過只是遺忘：不同的點餐名

再次閱讀上面的文章，完成下面的表格。

Q 完成表格。

Name	No. of meals	Names of meals	Time of meals
Monica	3	breakfast lunch supper	morning 12:30 8:30 or 9:30
Fred			
Mrs. Lockey			
David			
Jake			

解題

Name	No. of meals	Name of meals	Time of meals
Monica	3	breakfast lunch supper	morning 12:30 8:30 or 9:00
Fred	3	breakfast lunch supper	morning around 1:00 evening
Mrs. Lockey	4	breakfast dinner tea supper	around 8:30 about 1:00 around 5:30 about 10:00
David	2	lunch dinner	between 1:00 and 2:00 around 7:00
Jake	2	brunch dinner	about 11:00 evening

在填表格的時候，你有沒有發現什麼奇怪的地方呢？

大部分的人都是中午吃lunch（午餐），大概十二點或一點左右。然而，洛基太太卻把這一餐叫做dinner！有些人（莫妮卡與弗雷德）把晚餐叫做supper，但大衛和杰克卻把晚餐叫做dinner。洛基太太更奇怪，她的晚餐叫做tea，不過她的晚餐又比其他人都早吃。

這是因為她在睡前還要再吃一餐，這一餐叫做supper。與弗雷德的supper好像又不太一樣了。

☺ 絕對學過只是遺忘：**復習這些不同的餐名**

Q 完成下面這些句子。

① Everyone agrees that the meal in the morning is called _____.

② Most people eat _____ in the middle of the day.

③ _____ and _____ are the most common names for the main evening meal.

④ Some people eat _____ before they go to bed.

⑤ _____ is a combination of breakfast and lunch, eaten quite late in the morning (usually at weekends).

解題

① breakfast; ② lunch; ③ Supper, dinner; ④ supper; ⑤ Brunch

注意：在第3句和第5句中要填的單字是句子的開頭，所以第一個字母需要大寫。

☺ 絕對學過只是遺忘：**寫下你自己的飲食習慣**

Q 描述自己的飲食習慣。

寫三到四句話，描述自己的飲食習慣。如果你的飲食習慣和其他中國人都差不多，你可以用這樣的句型來展開句子：

Like most Chinese people, I ...

如果你的飲食習慣很不一樣，也可以改用這樣的句型：

Unlike most Chinese people, I ...

Q 把自己的飲食習慣寫下來吧!

請把它的題目標為:

<u>**Meals**</u>

_____

_____

_____

_____

_____

_____

_____

_____

_____

_____

_____

_____

_____

_____

_____

_____

Part 5—

讓你的英文能力起死回生！
關於不同的飲食文化

接下來我們就來更詳細地探討飲食習慣。

救回被遺忘的英文：關於世界各地的早餐

以下的清單列出了許多不同地方的人早餐會吃的食物。

Q 在這個清單中，勾出常見的中式早餐食物吧!

orange juice	waffles	fried dough sticks
fresh fruit	steamed buns/rolls	preserved bean curd
milk	eggs	cereal
bacon	pickled vegetables	toast
porridge	marmalade	jam
coffee	tea	yoghurt

解題

常見的中式早餐食物可能有：

milk（牛奶），porridge（粥），steamed buns/rolls（饅頭/花卷），eggs（蛋），cereal（麥片），pickled vegetables（醃菜），tea（茶），fried dough sticks（油條），preserved bean curd（豆腐乳），toast（烤麵包片），jam（果醬）。

不懂這些字的意思的話，可以查閱辭典。如果你早餐還有別的常吃的東西沒有在上面列出來，你也可以自己把它加上去。

沒有打勾的其他食物都是在美國、英國、澳洲等地常見的早餐食物。

 救回被遺忘的英文：如何聽懂一段討論彼此飲食習慣的對話

接下來，聽一段音檔！這段音檔的說話者是海倫與朱莉婭。還記得海倫嗎？她是理查德的女兒。海倫的媽媽和朱莉婭的媽媽是好朋友，朱莉婭星期六晚上到海倫家過夜。這段對話就發生在星期天的早上。

🔊 聽音檔，回答問題。 🔊 *Track 014*

❶ Which topics are discussed?
Tick the topics that Helen and Julia talk about:

breakfast	lunch
supper	getting up/waking up
boyfriends	staying up late at night

❷ What are the girls doing while they are chatting?
Tick the best description.

getting dressed	doing their hair
eating breakfast	washing the dishes

❸ Do you think anyone else is in the room with them? _____
(Write Yes or No.)

解題

❶ breakfast，lunch，getting up/waking up;

❷ eating breakfast 我們可以從朱莉婭一開始問了Do you always eat so much for breakfast?來判斷。最後海倫也說了You're eating lots today.，從她用的是現在進行式，可以判斷朱莉婭正在吃東西。

❸ No. 理論上房間裡應該沒有別人，因為海倫跟朱莉婭講了一個秘密。

救回被遺忘的英文：記住每種不同的食物名稱

　　現在我們已經知道，海倫和朱莉婭正在討論早餐和午餐。她們聊的是現在她們早餐或午餐都吃什麼食物，以及她們以前都吃些什麼食物。再聽一遍音檔，完成下面的表格。只需要把她們兩人提到的食物寫下來就好。如果還有時間，可以想想看：海倫的秘密到底是什麼呢？

🔊 聽音檔，完成表格。 🔈 *Track 014*

	Now	In the past
Helen	Breakfast: orange juice, ham... Lunch:	Breakfast: Lunch:

Julia	Breakfast: Lunch:	Breakfast: eggs, ham, tomatoes Lunch:

解題

你把全部食物都寫下來了嗎？我們先看看她們現在都吃些什麼吧！

For breakfast, Helen now has orange juice, ham and eggs, toast, jam, marmalade and coffee.

For lunch, Helen now has an apple and a few cookies.

For breakfast, Julia now has just cereal (or something).

For lunch, Julia now has a burger and fries (or something).

再來看看她們過去都吃些什麼。

Helen used to have toast and milk for breakfast.

She (Helen) used to have fast food for lunch.

Julia used to have ham, eggs, tomatoes (and so on) for breakfast.

She used to eat sandwiches (and so on) for lunch. (In other words, a packed lunch).

😀 **救回被遺忘的英文：如何使用used to來描述過去的習慣**

　　你或許已經注意到了在前面的解答中，在說明海倫與朱莉婭以前都吃什麼的時候，我們用到了以下句型：

Helen used to have toast and milk...

Julia used to have ham, eggs, tomatoes and so on...

　　在描述過去的習慣時，這是一個很常見的句型。在這段對話中，還可以找到很多使用這個句型的句子。聽聽看，寫下來。第一句已經幫你寫好了！

🔊 聽音檔，把含used to ...的句子寫下來。　◀ *Track 014*

❶ I used to eat a full cooked breakfast.

❷ _____ of my own accord.

❸ _____ eating breakfast.

❹ _____ and a quick cup of milk.

❺ _____ starving by lunchtime.

❻ _____ on lunch.

❼ _____.

❽ _____.

（小提示：第❼句與第❽句的內容是關於 packed lunches）

解題

2 I used to wake up of my own accord.

3 I used to hate eating breakfast.

4 I only used to have a piece of toast and a quick cup of milk.

5 I used to be starving by lunchtime.

6 I used to spend lots of money on lunch.

7 I used to take packed lunches to school.

8 She used to prepare the packed lunches for me before that.

你覺得第 **5** 句中的starving是什麼意思呢？是very tired，very poor，very rich 還是very hungry？沒錯，就是very hungry的意思。你應該可以猜到吧！她的 早餐吃得很少，所以到午餐時間就很餓。

救回被遺忘的英文：如何描述習慣上的改變

　　以下這些句子還沒有完成。我們可以從對話中聽出海倫和朱莉婭的飲食習慣 已經有了不小的改變。想想她們過去的習慣和現在的習慣各是什麼，完成下面的 句子。

完成下面的句子。　◀Track 014

我們先來寫寫海倫過去與現在的習慣。

1 Helen used to get up at the last minute but now _____.

2 She used to eat a quick breakfast but these days _____.

3 She used to spend lots of money on lunch but these days _____.

❹ She used to go to fast food restaurants but these days _____.

接下來是朱莉婭過去與現在的習慣。

❺ _____ but these days her dad has to wake her.

❻ _____ but these days she has something light like cereal.

❼ Julia's mum _____

but these days she allows her to eat a light breakfast.

❽ _____ but these days she eats in the school canteen.

解題

❶ she gets up early; ❷ she eats a lot at breakfast; ❸ she usually skips lunch; ❹ she always takes an apple and a few cookies with her and eats them in school; ❺ Julia used to wake up of her own accord; ❻ She used to eat a full, cooked breakfast; ❼ used to force her to eat a full, cooked breakfast; ❽ She used to take packed lunches to school

腦力激盪

想想看，你自己是不是也有一些習慣改變了呢？像是什麼時候起床，早餐和午餐吃什麼，在哪裡吃午餐等。請你也寫下幾個句子來談談自己吧！在寫的時候，可以唸唸看，並注意used to的發音方式（可以仔細聽音檔裡面外籍老師是怎麼唸的）。對了，開始使用這本書之後，你是不是也有一些習慣改變了呢？譬如：I used to have lots of free time but these days I'm always busy.（我以前很有空，但現在我總是很忙。）I used to watch TV in the evenings but these days I do language activities.（我以前晚上都在看電視，但現在我都在學習語言。）

😀 救回被遺忘的英文：找出每個詞的正確意思

在海倫和朱莉婭的對話中，或許有些單字或片語你聽不太懂。不用擔心，只要聽懂她們大概的意思，就能用推測來判斷一些單字的意思了。像是starving，你就已經猜到它的意思是very hungry。那接下來這些單字或片語，你能猜得出來是什麼意思嗎？如果需要的話可以再聽一次音檔，利用上下文語境來猜測單字的意思，並圈出最佳答案。

🔊 圈圈看，畫底線的單字或片語最可能是什麼意思？ ◀€*Track 014*

❶ I usually <u>skip lunch</u>.

      a) take exercise at lunchtime

      b) eat lunch

      c) miss lunch

      d) buy lunch

❷ I used to wake up <u>of my own accord</u>.

      a) without any help

      b) with the help of my alarm clock

      c) in my own bedroom

      d) with the help of a tape recorder

❸ ... but only <u>on special occasions</u>.

      a) occasionally

      b) during holidays

      c) at times for celebration

      d) at weekends

❹ I'm always <u>wide awake</u> ...

      a) completely awake

      b) feeling tired

c) far away

d) just opening my eyes

⑤ It was <u>too much hassle</u>.

a) too much paper

b) too heavy

c) too much trouble

d) too fattening

⑥ These waffles are <u>yummy</u>.

a) unpleasant

b) sticky

c) filling

d) delicious

解題

❶ c; **❷** a; **❸** c; **❹** a; **❺** c; **❻** d

注意！這是一段兩個十幾歲的少女之間的對話，所以她們才會用像skip lunch，hassle，yummy這種很不正式的字。其他的幾個字則比較正式一點，是隨時都可以用的。

對了，你聽出來海倫的秘密到底是什麼了嗎？沒錯，她都把午餐錢省下來去買CD了。以前人們會聽records（唱片），後來演變成tapes或cassettes（錄音帶）。現在人們會聽CD和MP3等。

Part 6──
讓你的英文能力起死回生！
看看萊恩在日常生活中的習慣

 救回被遺忘的英文：寫下每天早上應該做的事情

對你來說，普通的上班或上學日早上是什麼樣子呢？從你起來到出發去上班或上學，在這期間都做了什麼事情呢？大部分是個人的事還是家務事？把你做的最重要的事情寫在下面的橫線上。你有沒有做什麼很特別的事呢？有的話也要寫下來。

Q 寫出你每天早上必做的事。

① I get up. _____

② _____

③ _____

④ _____

⑤ _____

⑥ I leave for work/school. _____

 解題

你覺得你寫下來的內容和其他人會不會很類似呢？相信一定有很多相似的地方。無論是哪國人，早上一定都會做某些事吧，像是洗漱、穿衣服等！像我，在出門前還會澆澆花，這點可能是比較與眾不同的。

救回被遺忘的英文：如何透過雜誌報導來認識一個人

接下來，我們要讀一篇關於一名英國男子的雜誌報導。這本雜誌提供了一篇摘要，讓讀者可以快速知道整篇報導在講什麼。先看看這篇報導的標題和摘要吧！

閱讀報導的摘要，回答以下問題。

A. From the title we can predict that the article is going to describe:
- a) a very special day
- b) a day of problems
- c) an ordinary Sunday
- d) an ordinary working day

(tick the best answer)

B. Look at the introduction and decide whether these statements are true or false. Circle T (for true) or F (for false). Correct the false statements.

❶ Len works in Carswell, Manchester.	T	F
❷ He lives in a city.	T	F
❸ He is a family man.	T	F
❹ He and his wife have three teenage children.	T	F

JUST ONE OF THOSE DAYS!	**LEN ALLISON, 39, and his partner Alan Carswell, run a successful interior design company in South Manchester. Their work includes everything from designing a simple entrance hall to giving whole houses a "new look". Len and his wife, Wendy, recently moved to a large house in a Cheshire village. Their three children are Zoe, 14, Nicholas, 12 and Jason, 9.**

解題

你可以從這篇文章的標題看出什麼端倪呢？想必這篇文章描述的一定不是什麼特別的日子吧！光看just（只是）這個字，就知道這篇文章講的應該是很平常的一天，不是什麼充滿麻煩的一天，也不是周末。

從摘要中，我們可以看出萊恩在 Manchester（曼徹斯特）工作，不是卡斯韋爾（他工作伙伴的名字）。他住在 village（村莊）中，他是一個family man（有家室）。他的三個孩子並非都是teenage（十幾歲的），應該說He has three children.（他有三個孩子）才對。

答案：

A. d

B. ❶ F; ❷ F; ❸ T; ❹ F

😄 救回被遺忘的英文：如何快速瀏覽一篇文章並從中抓住重點

繼續閱讀這篇文章前，我們先來想想看：這篇文章可能會講什麼呢？如果讀的是中文文章，想必你應該從摘要中就可以猜到這篇文章的主旨了吧。發揮想像力，想一下文章要講什麼，對學習外語是很有幫助的。練習預測可以讓我們更容易了解一篇文章，並可以在閱讀過程中發現自己的預測是對還是錯。我想，你應該已經猜到了，這篇文章講的就是萊恩日常生活中天天做的事情！畢竟這是整個單元的主題！

這篇文章共有三個主要部分。在讀文章前，先猜猜看，這三個部分的主題可能是什麼呢？圈出下面最有可能的選項。

 選出最有可能的選項。

A. morning	B. before work	C. breakfast	D. travelling to work
aftcrnoon	work	lunch	work
evening	after work	dinner	travelling from work

現在就快速瀏覽一下整篇文章，你是否會改變主意呢？注意一定是快速瀏覽，不要逐字逐句地讀。

快速瀏覽　下整篇文章。

1. I usually wake just before seven and axxxxxx down to the kitchen to make tea — starting the day as a "good husband". I bxxxxx the newspapers from the doormat as I pass and get furious if the delivery boy is late! We get *The Guardian* and *The Mirror*. I cxxxxx through *The Mirror* while the kettle's boiling and find out about the latest royal family scandal. That usually puts a smile on my face.

2. By the time I get back upstairs with the tea tray, Wendy will be awake, grumbling about how long she's had to wait. After a few mouthfuls of tea, I go and kick the kids into the land of the living. It's not a dxxxxx I enjoy.

3. After a quick shower and shave, I exxxxx on some clothes — casual fxxxxx if we're having a day in the office, something gxxxxx if we're meeting clients. Alan's always complaining that I'm not smart enough. Clothes just don't interest me. I can't stand sportswear unless it's for sport and the recent trend for designer labels infuriates me. We're a typical Marks and Spencer family — but won't be for long because the kids are starting to rebel.

4. After breakfast, I drop the kids off at school and then hxxxxx into Manchester with all the other commuters. I swear at a few lorry drivers on the way. I always seem

to get stuck behind the biggest and slowest truck on the road and I'm always just that fractionally later than I would like to be — which provokes another moan from Alan as I walk into the office.

5. The office is a pleasant place to be in— except for Alan's complaints. We share all the work fairly evenly but Alan seems to think I always take the best jobs for myself. Not true. We've known each other for ever and ours has always been a love-hate relationship. I laugh at his ixxxxx and he laughs at my responses.

6. I enjoy our days in the office most of all. We'll sit at our drawing boards or our desks, working hard for a while and then jxxxxx for a chat. Alan will puff on his pipe at that point and I go round opening doors and windows to make him feel kxxxxx!

7. We listen to CDs while we work: jazz, classical, the Stones and the Beatles, Pink Floyd and the Velvet Underground, the sort of music that middle-aged people like us used to listen to on records when we were young. We drink cups of tea and coffee throughout the day and I eat my way through lxxxxx of sweets and chocolate bars. I'm always eating! Alan's being silly about his weight at the moment so he eats fruit. When my sweets run out, I'll mxxxxx an apple or two from his supplies and that will cause another squabble.

8. After a fair morning's work, we wander to the pub down the road for lunch. I normally have soup and then something meaty while Alan picks at a salad which wouldn't keep a rabbit happy. We both have our daily ration of beer, of course. We talk about work and our latest dreams of when we're millionaires. Football sometimes gets a mention too. Alan often tries to drag me into one of the antique shops we pass as we nxxxxx back to the office. He usually wins so he'll waste time examining an ugly pot and I'll look bored.

9. The afternoon passes pleasantly and I look forwards to the moment, usually around five, when Alan says "Well, that's it for today". I like him to make the first move!

10. The older children are usually glued to the TV when I get home but Jason will stop whatever he's doing to regale me with all his exciting news from school. I hang up my jacket and prepare for an evening of time-wasting — something I'm much better at than Wendy. She always has things to do.

11. We sometimes have a family dinner but more often than not, we eat after the kids have gone to their rooms so that we can try to talk to each other! My body always tells me I need to drink a few glasses of good wine. We rarely go out together because there's no one to babysit and, anyway, I get tired of oxxxxx restaurants since I take clients out quite often.

12. We may watch a bit of TV together at the end of the evening but we're often in bed with the papers by ten. Sleep always comes easily.

解題

正確答案是 B. before work, work and after work

救回被遺忘的英文：如何在快速瀏覽第二遍後判斷每段的大意

　　現在再快速看一下文章，判斷哪幾段談的是萊恩在工作前做的事、哪幾段談的是他在工作時做的事、哪些又是他下班後做的事。

Q 將段落的序號寫在下面的表格中。

Section	Para. No.
before work	
work	
after work	

現在要找出萊恩在哪幾段描述了用餐的事應該不難吧！在下表中，為每次的用餐填入段落序號。如果文章中沒有提到的，則畫個叉（×）。請注意，表格裡的**tea**指的是一次用餐的名稱（如洛基太太在**Part 4**中所說），並非可以喝的「茶」。

Topic	Para. No.
breakfast	
lunch	
tea	
dinner	
supper	

Which, if any, of Len's meals are described in detail? _____

解題

你在瀏覽這篇文章的時候，一定發現了一個奇怪的地方：為什麼有些單字裡面有一堆叉呢？別擔心，這些單字我們之後會在**Part 7**中再慢慢研究。

那麼你正確地找出描述萊恩日常生活事務的段落了嗎？

Before work: paragraphs 1,2,3 and 4;
Work: paragraphs 5,6,7,8 and 9;
After work: 10,11,12.
Breakfast: paragraph 4;
Lunch: paragraph 8;
Dinner: paragraph 11;
Tea and supper are not mentioned.

萊恩非常詳細地描寫了自己的午餐是什麼樣子。他也稍微描述了一下他的晚餐時間，不過他並沒有把他吃的東西寫出來。

 救回被遺忘的英文：如何在快速瀏覽第三遍後找出正確的資訊

除了了解萊恩都怎麼用餐以外，我們也可以從文章中稍微了解到他的飲食習慣。有哪幾段提到飲食呢？相信你應該很容易可以找出來吧！

閱讀所有提到萊恩飲食習慣的片段，然後在下頁的列表中勾出正確的敘述。

勾出正確的敘述。

1 Len likes eating and drinking.

2 Len's first drink of the day is coffee.

3 He's worried about his weight at the moment.

4 He often drinks beer and wine.

5 He never drinks alcohol.

6 He never eats anything in the office.

7 He likes both coffee and tea.

8 He's a vegetarian.

 解題

現在我們對萊恩的飲食習慣應該很了解了吧！第**1**、**4**、**7**句都是對的，其他則不正確。

 救回被遺忘的英文：如何在文章中找出需要的資訊

由以上的練習我們知道第**2**、**3**、**5**、**6**、**8**項敘述都不正確。為什麼呢？從文章中是不是可以找出一些句子來證明這些敘述不正確呢？

Q 將這些可以當作「證據」的句子寫在以下的橫線上（寫幾個單字把意思表達清楚即可）。

2 Len's first drink of the day is coffee.

... after a few mouthfuls of tea ...

3 He's worried about his weight at the moment.

5 He never drinks alcohol.

6 He never eats in the office.

8 He's a vegetarian.

解題

3 I'm always eating.（第7段）
5 We both have our daily ration of beer...（第8段）... I need to drink a few glasses of good wine.（第11段）
6 I eat ... sweets and chocolate bars.（第7段）
8 something meaty（第8段）

你猜猜看，萊恩會很瘦嗎？大概不是吧！你覺得他很在意自己的外表嗎？大概也不在意吧！

Part 7——
讓你的英文能力起死回生！
利用修辭技巧來描述生活習慣

　　現在相信你已經大概知道這整篇文章在講什麼了。我們接下來就要仔細看看裡面的用詞與語法！不過，在這之前，先了解一下以下這些與英國生活相關的文化元素。

第一段

newspapers from the doormat（門口踏腳墊上的報紙）：在英國，許多人都訂閱報紙，一早報紙就會被丟在家門口。

royal family scandal（皇室醜聞）：大部分的報紙都會提到英國皇室家族的醜聞。這些醜聞雖然可能略嫌有礙觀瞻，但許多人（例如萊恩）都很愛看。

第二段

kick the kids into the land of the living（把孩子踢進人世）：這是「把孩子叫醒」的幽默說法。kids是children的非正式說法。

第三段

a typical Marks and Spencer family（典型的M&S家族）：Marks and Spencer（M&S）是在英國及一些其他國家非常有名、非常受歡迎的連鎖店。這家店不但賣生鮮食品，也賣價格不貴但品質很好的衣服。萊恩說他家是「典型的M&S家族」，就表示他們家的人大部分的衣服都是從M&S買的。

第七段

the Stones and the Beatles, Pink Floyd and the Velvet Underground：這些都是樂團名，是二十世紀六七十年代非常受歡迎的樂團。

救回被遺忘的英文：如何聽懂他人抱怨的內容

　　這篇文章提到，溫蒂和艾倫都常抱怨萊恩的表現。第二段就提到溫蒂在grumbling，也就是「小小地抱怨一下」。第四段也用了moan這個單字，意思也是「小小抱怨一下」。第七段的squabble指的是「小吵一架或意見不合」。可以想像，有了moan或grumble，接下來就會發生squabble了！

　　溫蒂和艾倫到底在抱怨什麼呢？我們一起來看看。

Q 完成下列句子。

❶ Wendy complains because _____.

❷ Alan complains because _____.

❸ Alan complains because _____.

❹ Alan complains because _____.

❺ Alan complains because _____.

 解題

❶ she has to wait long for her morning tea

❷ Len is not smart enough

❸ Len arrives late at the office

❹ Len takes the best jobs for himself

❺ Len eats his apples

救回被遺忘的英文：如何運用**always**表述每次都想抱怨的事情

在這篇文章中，最常看到的時態就是一般現在式，其中也用了兩次現在進行式：

（第三段） Alan's **always** complaining that ...
（第七段） I'm **always** eating!

在這兩句中出現的**always**是用來強調句子中所闡述的事非常煩人或有點奇怪。我們常會使用這種句型來表示我們不太喜歡另一個人做的某些事，也就是使用這種句型表達我們的抱怨。

舉例來說，溫蒂抱怨萊恩時，她可能會對萊恩說：

You're always making me wait too long for my tea.

利用這個句型，想想看，艾倫在以下這些情境，會對萊恩說什麼呢？

Q 寫下艾倫可能會用來抱怨的句子。

❶ Alan complains that Len arrives late. He says:

_____

❷ Alan complains that Len takes the best jobs for himself. He says:

_____

❸ Alan complains that Len takes his fruit. He says:

_____

解題

❶ You're always arriving late.

❷ You're always taking the best jobs for yourself.

❸ You're always stealing my fruit.

腦力激盪

想像一下，如果你要對朋友或家人抱怨 些事情，你會怎麼用英文表達呢？

😊 救回被遺忘的英文：**如何挑選適當的辭彙去填補文章中的空白**

現在我們可以來看看這篇文章中使用的辭彙了。你會注意到雖然這篇文章中有15個壓淺灰色色塊的文字都畫了一堆叉，但你卻可以不管它們照樣了解文章的意思。可見有時我們根本不需要了解一篇文章中的所有單字，就可以看懂整篇文章。想想看，這些畫了叉叉的單字，可以用哪些單字（或兩個單字）來取代呢？在下一頁的空格中填入你覺得最適合的答案。

Q 寫下適合的單字，用來取代文章中畫了叉的單字。

a ____go____   b _____   c _____

d _____   e _____   f _____

g _____   h _____   i _____

j _____   k _____   l _____

m _____   n _____   o _____

解題

可能的答案有很多種，以下這些只是參考而已！
b collect/pick up/take/get; c look/glance; d job/task/chore;
e put; f things/clothes; g smart/neat; h go/drive/travel/hurry;
i criticisms/comments; j stop/break off;
k bad/guilty/uncomfortable/ashamed; l lots; m take/eat; n walk/go;
o expensive/good ...

救回被遺忘的英文：學一些非正式的表達方式

其實我在上面建議的解答與這篇文章中實際使用的表達不完全一樣。這是因為這篇文章為了達到某種效果，使用了不少特別的、口語化的表達。

閱讀下面的這些句子，或許你已經認識下面的一些單字了，不認識的單字則可以查閱辭典！想想看，為什麼這篇文章的作者要選擇使用這些畫底線的單字呢？

Q 思考一下，為什麼作者要使用這些畫底線的單字？

❶ I <u>flip</u> through *The Mirror* while the kettle's boiling ...（第一段）

❷ ... I <u>throw</u> on some clothes ...（第三段）

❸ ... casual <u>stuff</u> if we're having a day in the office ...（第三段）

❹ ... I eat my way through <u>mountains</u> of sweets and chocolate bars.（第七段）

❺ ... I'll <u>steal</u> an apple or two from his supplies ...（第七段）

❻ ... as we <u>wander</u> back to the office.（第八段）

解題

❶ flip 指的是快速翻閱一本讀物，這句是指萊恩並非仔細閱讀報紙，只是看看圖片、頭條新聞等。

❷ throw 指「丟」，是個非常快速又隨便的動作，這句指萊恩很快又很隨便地穿上衣服。

❸ stuff 是個非常不正式的詞，可用來指任何事物。在這句中表示萊恩不覺得衣服有什麼重要。

❹ mountains 是「山」，但萊恩真的吃了能堆成一座山那麼多的糖果嗎？當然沒有，這只是誇張的修飾法，表示他吃了很多。

❺ steal 指「偷」，但萊恩當然不是真的偷他同事的蘋果，他只是沒問就直接拿走而已。在這句中是幽默的用法。

❻ wander 是「閒逛；遊蕩」的意思，在這句中是表示萊恩和艾倫悠哉悠哉地慢慢回到辦公室去，可以讓我們感受到這兩個人對工作的態度是非常放鬆的。

小小一個單字，就可以表達好多意思。如果你現在還沒辦法使用這樣的單字表達誇張、幽默等各種效果，也沒關係！只要能夠看懂作者想表達的感覺就可以了。

😊 救回被遺忘的英文：**如何辨識出文章中的一般未來式**

前面我們提到了整篇文章中最常用到的時態就是一般現在式。不過，你是不是也注意到，有些句子用了will這個字呢？比如以下這句：

... Wendy <u>will</u> be awake.

除了這一句外，will還出現了很多次。再閱讀一次文章，把所有will出現的地方都標出來吧！

ⓆＱ 將文章中所有will出現的地方都畫上底線。

😊 救回被遺忘的英文：**如何解釋文章中使用will**

現在仔細看看所有你畫上底線的句子。想想看，為什麼要用到will（也就是未來式）呢？下面這些都是可能的理由。你覺得這篇文章的作者可能是為了以下哪些原因選擇使用will呢？把你覺得最可能的原因打勾（✓）。

Q 勾出你覺得作者在這篇文章中使用了will的原因。

1 to describe an action which is planned but which doesn't happen

2 to describe a future action

3 to describe a past routine

4 to describe a present routine

5 to describe an unplanned future action

6 to add variety to the text

7 to add a detail to a routine

8 to describe a casual part of a bigger routine

解題

在這篇文章中will跟將來一點關係都沒有，與過去更沒有關係，所以選項**1**、**2**、**3**、**5**都不對。在這篇文章中，will的用途是描述目前的習慣（選項**4**）、闡述細節（選項**7**）和描述一項習慣的其中一部分（選項**8**）。這篇文章中出現的「will+動詞」都可以直接用一般現在式替代，意思也不會改變。那到底為什麼要用will呢？因為要讓文章有點變化（選項**6**）！英文的時態真的好奇妙，對不對？

Part 8
讓你的英文能力起死回生！
請試著寫出一篇作文

學完這一單元，你就可以：

□ 描述你目前天天要做的事

□ 描述用餐狀況

□ 表達對各種習慣的感受

□ 描述過去天天要做的事

□ 詢問各種習慣

□ 表達輕微的不滿

對於萊恩的生活，你覺得有趣嗎？你對萊恩的個性了解多少？你對萊恩與艾倫的關係又了解多少呢？你覺得這篇文章有趣嗎？

現在請你再**復習**一下整個單元所做的練習，如果有什麼不了解的地方，可以和同學、朋友或老師一起討論！

救回被遺忘的英文：如何描述你日常生活中的一天

現在就請你寫一篇文章，描述你日常生活中的一天！你可以參考之前的文章，但不需要寫那麼長（250—300字即可）。請你寫三段：第一段說明你去上班或上學前固定會做的事；第二段說明你在上班或上學時固定會做的事；第三段說明你在下班或放學後會做的事。要記得，應該多使用一般現在式，不過也可以使用幾個will作為變化。

Q 將你日常生活中固定會做的事寫成一篇文章。

請給你的文章命名為這個標題：

Just One of Those Days

總復習

 令人擔心的情形

艾瑪不吃東西，她的媽媽墨芮太太很擔心，於是墨芮太太就去找醫生問問意見。

🔊 聽墨芮太太與醫生的對話，在下表中記下艾瑪過去與現在的習慣。 🔊 *Track 015*

	Before	**Now**
Weight		
Breakfast		
Lunch		
Dinner		
Drink		
Sport		

解題

	Before	**Now**
Weight	58 kilos	46 kilos
Breakfast	cereal and milk, a boiled egg with toast, tea with milk	a cup of black coffee, half a grapefruit
Lunch	school lunch — a full cooked meal	a few sticks of raw celery and carrot
Dinner	rice, potatoes or pasta with meat and vegetables	a salad — raw vegetables, a small piece of cheese or a thin slice of lean ham
Drink	milk, fruit juice	mineral water
Sport	lots, on school hockey team	none, no energy

Q 完成這個練習後,試試用自己的話描述一下艾瑪過去和現在的習慣有何不同。

例如:

She used to weigh 58 kilos, but now she only weighs 46.

題目如下：

Emma's Habits: Past and Present

_____

_____

_____

_____

_____

MP3音檔內容完整看

若是聽完音檔還是沒把握，建議可搭配本部份學習，不熟的語彙要查辭典並作筆記，方能加深英文記憶。

 Part 1: Track 012　　　（請配合140頁及音檔使用）

1. I get up early every day.

2. I don't mind getting up early.

3. I don't particularly like getting up early but I don't dislike it either.

4. I cook two meals every day.

5. I like cooking.

6. I dust the furniture once a week.

7. I don't like dusting.

8. I do the ironing twice a week.

9. I can't stand ironing.

 **Part 3: Track 013** （請配合153頁及音檔使用）

Richard:

I don't enjoy mornings at all. There are five of us in our house and only one bathroom. I usually take a bath at night to save time in the mornings. So, I get up at the last minute and just have a quick wash and shave. I have to shave in the mornings because I'm quite dark and hairy. Luckily, my wife usually gets up before me and organises breakfast. We all eat a big, cooked breakfast — though sometimes, the boys get up so late, they don't have time to eat anything. Occasionally, I have to literally drag them out of bed and then stay with them to make sure they wash and dress properly. They seem to hate hot water and, I don't understand it — they love wearing dirty clothes! We have five minutes of relative peace after the boys have left the house and then Helen spoils it by saying "Come on, Dad. It's time to leave".

Sara:

I don't like to rush in the mornings so I always get up quite early. I like to be able to tidy the house and prepare breakfast before the rest of the family is awake. Helen appears in the kitchen before everyone else — already showered and ready for school. She's a very organised person. She sometimes helps me prepare breakfast, if I'm lucky! I always cook breakfast for the whole family but we rarely all manage to sit down together. Helen and I usually have a quiet chat before the others join us, with the radio in the background. After the others have all left the house, I really enjoy the peace and quiet. I make all the beds and then I always do ten minutes' exercise. After that, I take a slow, hot shower. I choose my clothes for the day and then spend a while fixing my hair. After that, I feel ready to face the rest of the world.

Sam:

My brother and I always talk in bed at night so we never go to sleep until really late. Someone — usually Helen or Mum — always calls us in the mornings to try to wake us but we usually take no notice and just go back to sleep. My dad often has to drag us out of bed at the last minute! We then fight in the bathroom because we both need to use it at the same time. We always have to dress really quickly on school mornings and when we go down to the kitchen Mum often looks mad at us because we have no time to eat breakfast. She sometimes makes us go back upstairs to put on clean clothes and Helen comes to check on us. We don't like that! We leave the house before Dad and Helen because we have to catch the school bus at 8:15. We nearly always have to run to the bus stop — but, luckily, the bus always waits for us.

 Part 5: Track 014 　　　（請配合166頁及音檔使用）

Julia:　　Wow! Do you always eat so much for breakfast, Helen?

Helen:　　These days, I do. I always have orange juice, then ham and eggs, or something else cooked, and the toast and jam and marmalade ... and, of course, coffee.

Julia:　　Aren't you worried about getting fat?

Helen:　　Well, no. You see, these days, I usually skip lunch. Don't tell mum though. She gives me money to buy lunch at school but I never use it for lunch. I save it to buy CDs!

Julia:　　That's terrible! I always have lunch. In our house, we usually just have a quick, light breakfast — just cereal or something. I don't like eating a lot at breakfast time. It makes me feel sick. When I was younger, I used to eat a full, cooked breakfast — eggs, ham, tomatoes and so on — because my mum forced me to. She thought I needed it. But now we all agree that a light breakfast is much better. I think it's much more healthy. In fact my dad wakes me quite early these days, so there's enough time to relax while we eat. When I was little, I used to wake up of my own accord, but these days I'm always really tired.

Helen: I know what you mean. I used to hate eating breakfast — mainly because I used to hate getting out of bed! My dad used to call me a hundred times. I always arrived at the breakfast table at the last minute so there was no time to eat much ... and I only used to have a piece of toast and a quick cup of milk. My mum was always saying "breakfast is the most important meal of the day. You should eat more". She was right ... I used to be starving by lunchtime. So, I used to spend lots of money on lunch. I always went to one of those fast food places near school. You know how expensive they are!

Julia: I very occasionally go to a fast food restaurant at lunchtime these days — but only on special occasions. You know, if it's a friend's birthday or something. But we're lucky. Our school canteen is quite good and cheap, so I usually eat there and have a burger and fries or something.

Helen: But think of all the money you spend! I really like this new arrangement. I get up early and help Sara prepare breakfast and then we chat while we eat and usually listen to the radio. It's really good. And I'm always wide awake by the time I leave for school.

Julia: But don't you feel hungry at lunchtime?

Helen: No, not really. I always take an apple and a few cookies with me and eat them in school.

Julia: I used to take packed lunches to school — sandwiches and so on. But when I had my fourteenth birthday, my mum said I had to start making the sandwiches myself. She used to prepare the packed lunches for me before that. I tried once or twice but it took me too long. It was too much hassle.

Helen: Hey! You say you don't like eating a lot at breakfast time but you're eating lots today!

Julia: Yes. I know but today's Sunday and it's already 10 o'clock. We often have big breakfasts at home on Saturdays and Sundays when there's plenty of time. Umm ... These waffles are yummy. Your mum ... I mean Sara ... is a really great cook, isn't she?

Helen: I guess so. She's pretty good at everything. My dad's a lucky guy. In fact, I'm lucky too. Do you think I should tell Sara that I don't use my lunch money to buy lunch?

 總復習聽力原文：Track 015　（請配合194頁及音檔使用）

Doctor: Good morning, Mrs. Murray. How are you?

Mrs. Murray: Good morning, doctor. Fine, thank you. I've not come to see you about me. There's nothing wrong with me ... well ... except worry. That is ... you see, it's my daughter, Emma.

Doctor: Oh, yes. Emma must be ...15 now. Is that right?

Mrs. Murray: She's just turned 16 actually.

Doctor: And what's the problem?

Mrs. Murray: Well, she just won't eat. She thinks she's too fat and keeps dieting to lose weight, but she's so thin now that it's getting really worrying.

Doctor: I see, well ... let me just get Emma's file ... Ah, yes, I remember when Emma came to see me a year ago, I weighed her ... Let's see ... she was 58 kilos then, which for a girl of 1 metre 69 is not too heavy. How much does she weigh now?

Mrs. Murray: Oh, she's well under 50 kilos now. I think it's about 46.

Doctor: Mm ... what about her eating habits, Mrs. Murray? Tell me what she eats every day.

Mrs. Murray: Well, she used to have a really healthy breakfast ... cereal and milk, and a boiled egg with toast, tea with milk ... but now she just has a cup of black coffee and half a grapefruit. I just can't get her to eat more.

Doctor: Yes, that's not much to start the day with. What about lunch?

Mrs. Murray: Well, she's stopped having school lunches. You know, she used to eat a full cooked meal at school, but now she just takes some sticks of raw celery and carrot.

Doctor: That's all?

Mrs. Murray: Yes. I've tried to make sandwiches for her, but she won't eat bread or butter. She says they're too fattening.

Doctor: Oh dear. Well, does she have a proper meal for dinner?

Mrs. Murray: No, instead of the meals that she always used to eat with us ... you know, we usually have rice, potatoes or pasta with meat and vegetables ... she now has only a salad, raw vegetables and sometimes a very small piece of cheese, or one thin slice of lean ham. She eats almost no meat now.

Doctor: Does she drink anything during the day?

Mrs. Murray: Not really, just mineral water. She refuses to drink milk or fruit juice, which she always used to.

Doctor: What about sports, Mrs. Murray? I remember Emma was very good at sports and used to do a lot at school. Wasn't she on the school hockey team?

Mrs. Murray: Yes, that's right, but not anymore. She stopped about six months ago. Her games teacher told me that Emma just doesn't seem to have any energy anymore. So, now she doesn't do any sports. She just seems so tired all the time.

Doctor: Well, I'm not surprised with a diet like that. This sounds like a classic case of anorexia nervosa, Mrs. Murray. Do you know what that is?

Mrs. Murray: Well, I know that it's common amongst girls of her age, but I thought she would grow out of it.

Doctor: I'm afraid it's more serious than that. She could be suffering from malnutrition — she's just not getting what her body needs from food. Emma seriously needs professional help. I think we'll have to get her to a psychiatrist. It would be best if you could get her in to see me first and let me talk to her about the seriousness of her condition.

Mrs. Murray: Oh dear. I'll do my best to get her in to see you, doctor.

Unit 4 出遊 Getting Around

Unit 4 出遊

Getting Around

有些人是「路痴」，而有些人天生方向感就比較好，就算到了完全陌生的環境，還是一樣找得到路。你呢？你的方向感怎樣？如果要描述路線、地點等，你的英文能力夠好嗎？如果外國人問你路，你能幫他/她指路嗎？學完這個單元，你就能成功地用英文問路、指路了！

 來個小暖身：如何找到正確的地理位置

看看下面這些句子。把每一句的順序排好，就能排列出一個簡短的對話，其中一方在問另一方資訊。排列完成後判斷一下此對話的主題是什麼。

▶將句子重新排列組成對話，並判斷此對話的主題。

> You're welcome.

> Do you know where there is a phone?

> Yes. There's one beside the main gate.

> Thank you very much.

> Excuse me.

Now write the words from the speech bubbles in the appropriate places below.

A: _____

B: _____

A: _____

B: _____

The topic of the conversation is:

A. the location of the main gate

B. the location of a telephone

C. how to use a telephone

D. the time

E. the cost of a telephone call

解題

希望這個簡單的暖身讓你對這個單元的主題已經有點概念了！這段對話的主題當然就是 "the location of a telephone"（電話的位置）了。
句子的順序為：

A: Excuse me. Do you know where there is a phone?
B: Yes. There's one beside the main gate.
A: Thank you very much.
B: You're welcome.

　　抵達一個完全陌生的地方時，我們有幾種選擇：冒著迷路的風險硬闖、看地圖或問路。你喜歡哪一種呢？

一般的地圖或示意圖都會將一些常見的重要建築、設施等以符號或圖片的形式標出。我們在下面列出了一些地圖或示意圖上可能看得到的符號或圖片。將這些符號或圖片與其最有可能代表的地點或設施搭配起來，把正確的單字或片語寫在每個符號或圖片下面的空格中。

▶ 將適當的單字或片語填入每個符號或圖片下面的空格中。

| restaurant | post office | telephone | bank | hospital |
| supermarket | main road | hotel | park | side road |

 解題

❶ supermarket; ❷ hospital; ❸ bank; ❹ restaurant; ❺ telephone;
❻ post office; ❼ main road; ❽ side road; ❾ park; ❿ hotel

Part 1——
10年英語不白學！
如何在陌生環境中找出準確的位置

在這個練習中（以及本單元後面的其他部分），我們會遇到大衛‧費伊，一個來到北京外國語大學的客座專家。大衛一年前才來到中國，所以你應該可以想像很多事他都還不太習慣。幸好北京外國語大學的外交事務代表金洪在機場接了大衛，並把他帶到他的住所。

 絕對學過只是遺忘：如何獲取基本資訊

金洪把大衛帶到住所後，給了他一份北京外國語大學校園及周邊環境的簡單介紹並告訴他還會有一場歡迎晚宴，如果他有什麼問題，可以在那時候詢問。

看看下面這份北京外國語大學的簡介，並把其中提到的所有設施都畫上底線。想像一下，哪些設施是大衛應該要知道的並且以後可能會用到的呢？我已經替你畫出了兩個作為範例。

Text 1
Welcome to Beijing Foreign Studies University!

Beijing Foreign Studies University (BFSU) is situated in the north-west of Beijing, in Haidian District. There are several other <u>universities</u> and <u>colleges</u> in the district, in addition to a wide range of offices, shops, restaurants and other facilities. The Friendship Hotel and the Shangri-La Hotel are nearby.

BFSU has two campuses, separated by the Third Ring Road: the East Campus and the West Campus. There is a convenient underpass between the two campuses. Most academic departments, their offices and classrooms are situated on the East Campus, as well as students' dormitories and the library. Some foreign experts, teachers and students live on the West Campus. The West Campus also has a number of small shops, restaurants and a fruit and vegetable market. There is also a bicycle repair workshop where it is possible to buy second-hand bicycles. You can choose to shop on the campus itself or take advantage of the facilities outside the campus gate.

Within no more than ten minutes' walk from the gate, you can find a news-stand, a flower shop, a beauty salon and a post office.

The university is some twelve miles, or a one and a half hours' bus ride, from the centre of Beijing. There are convenient bus stops near the campus gate. You can also take the bus to other parts of Beijing and make shorter journey within the Haidian area. Taxis are usually parked at the university gate. As you will see, many people use bicycles rather than other forms of transportation.

We hope your stay in Beijing is successful and rewarding. Please don't hesitate to contact your foreign affairs representative if you require any further information or have any problems.

解題

提到的設施有：offices, shops, restaurants, the Friendship Hotel, the Shangri-La Hotel, the Third Ring Road, the East Campus, the West Campus, an underpass, academic departments, office buildings, students' dormitories, library, a fruit and vegetable market, a bicycle repair workshop, a news-stand, a flower shop, a beauty salon, a post office, bus stops

 絕對學過只是遺忘：如何挑選出重要的資訊

　　如果拿到一份像上面這樣的材料，你又沒有時間從頭讀到尾，那麼能從長長的文件中挑出需要的資訊的能力就顯得格外重要了。下面的表格可以幫你實現這個目標！現在再閱讀一遍這份介紹，把其中的資訊分成不同的類別，填好下面的表格。每個空格只要填一兩個字就可以了！

Q 閱讀簡介，完成下面的表格。

Location:
　　　　part of Beijing: northwest
　　　　name of area: Haidian
Campus:
　　　　number of campuses:　＿＿＿＿＿＿＿＿＿＿＿＿
　　　　names of campuses:　＿＿＿＿＿＿＿＿＿＿＿＿

divided by: _____

linked by: _____

Buildings:

   buildings on the East Campus _____

_____

   buildings on the West Campus _____

_____

Other facilities on the West Campus: _____

Facilities outside the campus gate: _____

_____

Suggested forms of transportation: _____

_____

解題

共有兩個校區：東校區與西校區。兩個校區中間有一條三環路，之間以地下道相通。大部分的系所、辦公室與教室都在東校區，學生宿舍、圖書館也都在那裡。有些外國專家、老師與留學生宿舍在西校區，而西校區還有一些小店、餐廳、蔬果店以及自行車維修中心。校門外還有更多設施，因為這所大學離市中心不是很遠，要到別處去的話可以搭公車、計程車，當然也可以騎自行車。根據這些提示，很容易就寫出答案了。

絕對學過只是遺忘：判斷提到的各種資訊

前面的簡介就是一種所謂的introductory leaflet，即提供資訊的單子。這種單子有很多不同的形式，也可能含有各式各樣的資訊。一些較常見的資訊種類都列在下面了。看一看，把和北京外國語大學（BFSU）相關的、在簡介中提到的資訊都打勾（√）。

Q 把簡介中提到的資訊打勾（√）。

❶ the history of the school

❷ the location

❸ the important places nearby

❹ the number of teachers and students

❺ the size of the campuses

❻ the facilities within the campus

❼ the courses offered by different departments

❽ the length of the semesters

❾ the distance from the city centre

❿ the sports facilities

⓫ transportation available

⓬ plans for improvement

解題

提到的資訊：❷ the location; ❸ the important places nearby; ❻ the facilities within the campus; ❾ the distance from the city centre; ⓫ transportation available

☺ 絕對學過只是遺忘：哪些才是描述地點的常用句型

雖然各個地點的描述可能會有不小的區別，但句型通常卻很類似。最常見的句型有：

It is ...　　　　It has ...

There is ...　　There are ...

閱讀前面的簡介，從中挑出符合以上這些句型的例句，各兩句。

Ⓠ 為以上句型各挑出兩句例句。

It is ...

1. _____

2. _____

It has ...

1. _____

2. _____

There is ...

1. _____

2. _____

There are ...

1. _____

2. _____

那You can ... 算不算是重要的句型呢？沒錯，是的！現在也在簡介中找到兩句使用這個句型的例句吧！這個句型通常用來提供額外的資訊。

You can ...

1. _____

2. _____

Why do you think the writer chose to use "You can ..." instead of "It is possible to ..."? Write your suggestion below.

_____.

解題

我想你的答案對不對，應該自己就能看出來了吧！為什麼我們要加入You can ... 這個句型呢？這是因為它可以讓整個簡介內容的語氣更友善親密，更能表達出歡迎對方的感覺。

絕對學過只是遺忘：如何正確地描述特定地點

目前我們已經學習了各種不同的資訊種類，以及最常用來描述地點的句型。你以後也可能會遇到要到你學校或工作地點的外國訪客。現在就請你參考之前的那份北京外國語大學的簡單介紹，寫一份簡短的介紹或「歡迎單」吧！寫在你的練習本上就行了。以下還有一份清單，列出所有你應該要寫到的資訊種類，以及需要用到的句型。

寫一份「歡迎單」，歡迎別人來到你的學校或工作地點。

Checklist	
Types of information	**Types of sentence structure**
location	
important places nearby	It is ...
campus	It has ...
buildings	There is ...
facilities within the campus	There are ...
facilities outside the gate	You can ...
distance from city centre	
transportation	

一旦你覺得滿意了，就可以把它抄到作業本上。請使用這個標題：

Welcome to Our School/Company

Part 2——
10年英語不白學！
如何提供簡單又精確的指示

 絕對學過只是遺忘：提供簡單的指示

　　還記得嗎？Unit 2中，安和菲利普辦了一場喬遷派對。當菲利普在指引客人到他們要去的房間（例如廚房）時，他用了the second room on the left（左邊第二間）。他還用了go straight ahead（直走），turn right（右轉）。

　　大衛來到這所學校後沒多久，就打算繞著校園慢慢散步，以便熟悉周邊環境。想像一下，假設你就站在東校區大門口，你要怎麼指點大衛呢？大聲說出來吧！一定要記得，如果想提高口語能力，就一定要多練習說才行。別忘了，你應該說the second building on the left，而不是學菲利普說the second room on the left，因為你現在是在學校裡，不是在家裡。

 看地圖，提供到以下這些地方的指示。

a. playground   b. library

c. administrative building   d. gymnasium

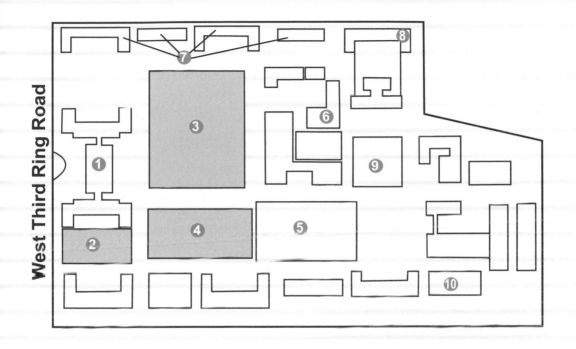

West Third Ring Road

1. main building
2. garden
3. playground
4. tennis court
5. gymnasium
6. English Department
7. students' dormitories
8. administrative building
9. library
10. canteen

解題

先繼續做第二個和第三個練習吧！因為這三題彼此有密切的關聯。從這兩個練習的「解題」處，你可以得到一些啟發。

絕對學過只是遺忘：如何判斷描述是否正確

參考地圖，判斷一下下面這些描述是正確的還是錯誤的。在正確的描述前寫下T，在錯誤的前面寫下F。第一題已經為你寫好了！

Q 判斷以下描述是否正確。

(T) ❶ If you go through the main building which is opposite the entrance of the East Campus, you can see the playground.

( ) ❷ If you turn right as you enter the gate of the East Campus and walk straight ahead, you can see a garden on your left.

( ) ❸ If you go through the garden, you will see the library in front of you.

解題

第❶、❷項描述正確。

第❸項描述應為：If you go through the garden, you will see the tennis court in front of you.

絕對學過只是遺忘：如何問路/指路

閱讀下面的簡短對話，並完成後面的練習。在練習時，請先寫下對話中出現過的用詞，再加入其他你想得到的說法。

Q 閱讀下面的對話，並完成練習。

A：Excuse me. Could you tell me where the post office is, please?

B：Yes, of course. You go out of the main gate and turn left. Walk about two hundred metres and you will see it on your left.

A：That sounds easy enough. Thanks a lot.

B：You're welcome.

Asking for/Giving directions.

❶ To draw a stranger's attention, you can say: _____

or _____

❷ To ask for directions, you can say: _____

_____

or _____

or _____

❸ To give directions, you can use: _____

_____

or _____

and _____

❹ To express thanks, you can say: _____

or _____

or _____

❺ To respond to the thanks, you can say: _____

or _____.

解題

❶ 要引起陌生人的注意，我們會用：
Excuse me ...（不好意思……）或 I wonder if you can help me ...（不知道你可不可以幫我……）。

❷ 要問路時，我們會用：
Could you tell me where ... is?（你可以告訴我……在哪裡嗎？），I'm looking for ... Do you know where it is (they are)?（我在找……，你知道在哪裡嗎？）或 Do you happen to know where ...?（你知不知道……在哪裡？）或 Where is the ...?（……在哪裡？）。

❸ 要提供指示時，我們會用：
「You + 動詞原形」或直接使用祈使句 Go straight ahead and then turn left ...（你就直走然後左轉……），最後再加上一句陳述句，如 It's on the left.（就在左邊。）或 You'll see it on your left.（你會在左手邊看到它。）。

❹ 要表示感謝時，我們會用：
Thanks a lot.（非常感謝。），Thank you very much (indeed).（真的很感謝你。），Many thanks.（多謝。）或 Thanks for your help.（謝謝你的幫忙。）。

❺ 要回應別人的感謝，我們會用：
You are welcome.（不客氣。），My pleasure.（我很樂意。）或 Not at all.（沒什麼。）。

Part 3——
10年英語不白學！
各式各樣的地標

 絕對學過只是遺忘：如何描述地標

　　問路時，人們有時候會提到地標（**landmark**）。你會描述地標嗎？以下有五棟建築的圖片，請從下面選出最適合各圖的描述。

Q 在每張圖片旁寫下適當的描述。

a building with a ramp up to the front door

a building with a table and chairs outside

a building with plants on either side of the front door

a building with a sloping roof

a building with a pavilion on the top

❶ This is a _____
_____ .

❷ This is a _____
_____ .

❸ This is a _____
_____.

❹ This is a _____
_____.

❺ This is a _____
_____.

也將圖6—10寫下類似的描述吧！可以使用以下這些單字：dome（拱頂），flat（平坦的），steps（階梯），chimneys（煙囪）。如果有哪個單字不了解，可以查閱辭典。

 寫下描述這些建築的句子。

6 This is a _____
_____.

7 This is a _____
_____.

8 This is a _____
_____.

9 This is a _____
_____.

⑩ This is a _____
_____ .

🤖 解題

❶ This is a building with a pavilion on the top.

❷ This is a building with a table and chairs outside.

❸ This is a building with a sloping roof.

❹ This is a building with a ramp up to the front door.

❺ This is a building with plants on either side of the front door.

❻ This is a building with steps up to the front door.

❼ This is a building with chimneys.

❽ This is a building with a dome on the top.

❾ This is a building with a flat roof.

❿ This is a building with a cross.

絕對學過只是遺忘：如何讀懂別人的留言

　　大衛在校園內逛了一圈，回到他住的外國專家大樓時，在信箱裡找到了一張留言。他發現是一位在北京的一家英國公司工作的朋友喬納森寫的。以下是喬納森寫的留言。如你所見，留言中說明了如何到喬納森住的旅館。閱讀這份留言，並完成下面的表格。

Text 2

Hello, David,

　　I imagine you've now had time to settle down. It would be great to see you. Why not come to my hotel and have a beer one evening? It's quite near your university.

　　You can get here easily by bus or bike. You go south from Weigongcun — either on bus 332 or on your bike. You pass the National Library of China. You can see a grand white building with steps in front and then Black Bamboo Park — the park with lots of bamboo growing inside the walls. You turn left immediately after the park. You'll see the Capital Stadium on your left. Go straight ahead and then turn right when you see a tall building with a revolving hexagonal restaurant on the top — the Xiyuan Hotel. You get off the bus at the stop after the Xiyuan Hotel (if you decide to come by bus). You carry on going south for about 500 metres and then, on your left, you will see my hotel — the Xindadu Hotel. I'm in room 2507.

Call me to let me know which evening to expect you (8453388 — 507).

　　Looking forwards to seeing you soon.
　　Regards,
　　Jonathan

閱讀留言，完成表格。

The hotel Jonathan lives in:	
His room number:	
Distance from BFSU:	
Suggested means of transport:	

 解題

Jonathan lives in the Xindadu Hotel.

His room number is 2507.

The hotel is quite near BFSU.

By bus or by bike.

 絕對學過只是遺忘：找出一封信件中的重點

　　大衛決定搭公車去見喬納森。看完信後，他做了筆記，用來提醒自己如何前往。請幫大衛完成下面的筆記吧！

請完成大衛的筆記。

Jonathan's place: The (a) _____ Hotel   (Room (b) _____)

Bus No.: (c) _____, south from (d) _____.

Pass (e) _____

　　(f) _____

Turn (g) _____

Go (h) _____

Turn (i) _____ at (j) _____

Get off (k) _____

Walk (l) _____

Hotel (m) _____

解題

ⓐ Xindadu; ⓑ 2507; ⓒ 332; ⓓ Weigongcun; ⓔ the National Library of China; ⓕ Black Bamboo Park; ⓖ left after the park; ⓗ straight ahead; ⓘ right; ⓙ the Xiyuan Hotel; ⓚ at the stop after the Xiyuan Hotel; ⓛ 500m south; ⓜ on the left

😀 絕對學過只是遺忘：哪些才是描述地點的常用句型

前面學習了一個簡單但非常實用的句型：

This is ... with ...（This可換為It）

使用這個句型將以下的句子結合起來。不需要把答案寫下來，大聲唸出來就可以了。

Ⓠ 將句子結合起來，並大聲唸出。

❶ This is a brand-new building. There are coloured flags in front of it.

❷ It is a small shop. But there are lots of neon lights on the roof.

❸ This is a big department store. There is a parking lot in front of it.

❹ It is a two-storey building. There is a big advertisement on the top.

❺ It's a newly-opened beauty salon. There are several baskets of flowers outside.

解題

❶ This is a brand-new building with coloured flags in front of it.

❷ It is a small shop with lots of neon lights on the roof.

❸ This is a big department store with a parking lot in front of it.

❹ It is a two-storey building with a big advertisement on the top.

❺ It's a newly-opened beauty salon with several baskets of flowers outside.

Part 4 —
10年英語不白學！
準確地聽取所需的資訊

 絕對學過只是遺忘：如何抓準主題

音檔中的這段對話是大衛打電話給金洪尋求幫助的。聽音檔回答這些問題，不用寫完整的句子，只要寫下的字能夠表達你的意思即可。

🔊 聽音檔，回答問題。 ◀Track 016

1 What has David just received?

_____

2 What sort of information does he want from Jin Hong?

_____

3 What is David's destination?

_____

4 Jin Hong mentions three possible ways of getting there. What are they?

_____

5 How does David decide to travel?

_____

6 Why does David choose this form of transport rather than the other two possibilities?

_____

_____

解題

❶ He has received an invitation to a party from the British Council.

❷ He wants information about how to get there.

❸ His destination is the Landmark Hotel.

❹ She mentions going by bike, by bus or by taxi.

❺ He decides to travel by taxi.

❻ He chooses to go by taxi because it's more comfortable than an ordinary bus and he doesn't have a bike (so he can't cycle there!).

這家旅館的名字很有趣,就叫Landmark!看來旅館的主人很希望他的旅館成為一個真正的地標(landmark)。

😊 絕對學過只是遺忘:如何詢問所需的資訊

　　既然大衛打電話給金洪是為了詢問一些資訊,也難怪這個對話都是一堆問題和答案了。聽音檔,寫下大衛確切問了哪些問題。

🔊 聽音檔,寫下大衛問的問題。 ◀ *Track 016*

Q❶ _____

Q❷ _____

Q❸ _____

Q❹ _____

Q**⑤** _____

Q**⑥** _____

Q**⑦** _____

Q**⑧** _____

 解題

大衛問的問題如下：

Q**❶** : Could you spare me a minute or two?

Q**❷** : Can you tell me the best way to get to the hotel?

Q**❸** : Is there a direct bus to the hotel?

Q**❹** : Where should I get off?

Q**❺** : How often do the buses run?

Q**❻** : How long does it take?

Q**❼** : What is the fare if I take the bus?

Q**❽** : And if I take a taxi?

寫下問題時，你會發現這些問題都很直接。這是因為大衛現在和金洪比較熟了，所以不用再問得那麼客氣。而且他也不想占用她太多時間！

請注意，最後一個問題 (Q**❽**) 並不符合正常的問句語法規則。

😊 絕對學過只是遺忘：如何提供所需的資訊

現在請你寫下金洪給大衛的答覆。不用詳細抄下所有細節，基本的答案就足夠了。

 寫下金洪對於這些問題的答覆。

_____

_____

_____

_____

_____

_____

解題

Q❶ : You needn't be that polite.

Q❷ : It's quite a long way but it's an easy journey. You'll have to take a bus.

Q❸ : Yes.

Q❹ : At Liangmaqiao Station.

Q❺ : I'm not sure but probably about every 15 minutes.

Q❻ : Well, about one hour and 15 minutes.

Q❼ : About two *yuan*.

Q❽ : No more than fifty *yuan*.

😀 絕對學過只是遺忘：還有其他更實用的問題

大衛與金洪的對話非常直接，可能還有一些問題他忘了問。以下列出一些關於公車的實用問題，而後面方框內也寫下了可能的答案。試著把答案和題目搭配起來吧！把最可能的答案字母寫在橫線上。有些題目可能不只一個答案！我已經為你做好第一題了！

Q 將問題與答案搭配起來。

❶ Where is the nearest bus stop? ___j___

❷ Is this the bus to the Landmark Hotel? _____

❸ How much is the fare? _____

❹ Where does the bus leave/go from? _____

❺ How many stops is it to the hotel? _____

❻ How long does it take? _____

❼ Where should I change for the Landmark Hotel? _____

❽ How often do the buses run? _____

❾ Can you tell me where to get off? _____

❿ Do I have to change anywhere? _____

⓫ Does this bus go past the station? _____

⓬ Is there any kind of bus timetable? _____

a. One *yuan*.

b. Every ten minutes.

c. About half an hour.

d. Yes, it is.

e. About 10.

f. Yes. You have to change to bus 302 at Renmin University.

g. Renmin University.

h. No, it doesn't.

i. It's not far.

j. Just round the corner.

k. Yes, you can.

l. No, you don't need to change.

m. No, you have to take bus 323.

n. No, I'm sorry.

o. Yes, with pleasure.

解題

❷ d, n;   ❸ a;   ❹ g, j;   ❺ e;   ❻ c;
❼ g;   ❽ b;   ❾ o;   ❿ f, l;   ⓫ h, m;   ⓬ n

絕對學過只是遺忘：如何完成一段包含詢問及提供資訊的對話

用適當的問題或回答完成以下對話。可以使用前面練習中的問題與答案！

Q 完成對話。

A1: _____

B1: The Normal University? It's not far so _____

A2: But I've lent my bike to someone. I thought of going by bus or taxi.

B2: There's no need to go by taxi. _____

A3: _____

B3: Bus 508.

A4: _____

B4: It goes from the stop across the road from the main gate of the Science and Technology University. You know where I mean?

A5: Yes, sure. _____

B5: Quite regularly, I think.

A6: _____

B6: No. That one will drop you right opposite the Normal University.

A7: _____

B7: I'm not sure but certainly no more than 2 *yuan*.

A8: _____

B8: Not many — probably about six or seven. It's not far at all.

A9: Right. I think I can probably manage. Thanks a lot. I'll see you later.

解題

下面只列出一些最常見的問問題與提供資訊的方式:

A1: What's the best way to get to the Normal University?

B1: you could go by bike.

B2: You can take the bus./You can go by bus.

A3: Which bus should I take?

A4: Where does it go/leave from?

A5: How often do the buses run?

A6: Do I need to change?

A7: How much does it cost?

A8: How many stops are there?

 絕對學過只是遺忘:如何說出日常生活中用得到的指示

想像一下,如果有個外國人從另一個城市來看你,那他/她可能得從公車或火車站到你家吧!他/她可能會問你哪些問題呢?你要怎麼跟他/她說明如何搭公車以及公車多久來一班等問題呢?接下來再想像一下,假如你要去拜訪住得很遠的朋友,你會問哪些問題呢?大聲說說看!

Q 練習詢問並回答和交通方式相關的問題。

Part 5——
讓你的英文能力起死回生！
各式各樣的交通方式

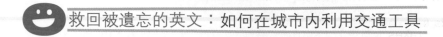 救回被遺忘的英文：如何在城市內利用交通工具

在一個城市中，有哪些交通方式呢？把可能的交通方式寫在下面的橫線上。

Q 寫出在城市中的交通方式。

People can go:

      by bus   _____

_____   _____

_____   _____

_____   _____

_____   _____

解題

交通方式有：by bus (minibus)（公共汽車或小型公共汽車），by tram（電車），by trolleybus（電車），by taxi（計程車），by underground（地鐵），by motorbike（摩托車），by bicycle/bike（自行車），by tricycle（三輪車），by motor tricycle（電動三輪車），on foot（步行）。

注意：搭乘各種交通工具用的是by這個介系詞，步行用的是on foot。

😀 救回被遺忘的英文：認識自行車的各個部位

自行車是一種受歡迎的交通方式。很多人都騎自行車去上學、上班或出遊。我想你應該也有一輛常騎的自行車吧！

你知道自行車的各個部位叫什麼名字嗎？你或許知道seat（座椅），bell（車鈴），wheel（車輪），tyre（車胎），chain（鏈子），但你知道crossbar（橫桿），brakes（刹車），spoke（輪輻），pedal（踏板），mudguard（擋泥板），reflector（反光板），handlebar（把手）嗎？

把以下單字與其定義搭配起來，並把正確的字母寫在定義前面。

Q 把單字與定義搭配起來。

a. pedal	b. spoke	c. valve	d. rim	e. reflector
f. mudguard	g. handlebar	h. crossbar	i. brakes	

(　　) ❶ the edge of a wheel on which a tyre is fitted

(　　) ❷ a part attached to the tyre for controlling the flow of air

(　　) ❸ the horizontal metal on a man's or boy's bicycle

(　　) ❹ a curved cover over a wheel of a bicycle

(　　) ❺ a bar with a handle at each end for steering a bicycle

(　　) ❻ the equipment for slowing or stopping the bicycle

(　　) ❼ one of the two pats which the cyclist presses with the feet to make the bike move

(　　) ❽ a small circle/piece of plastic that is usually fitted to the back of a bicycle to reflect light

(　　) ❾ one of the very thin metal bars that connect the centre of a wheel to its outer edge

解題

① d; ② c; ③ h; ④ f; ⑤ g; ⑥ i; ⑦ a; ⑧ e; ⑨ b

救回被遺忘的英文：分辨自行車的各個部位

你知道前面練習中提到的這些自行車的部位長什麼樣子嗎？把正確的名字填入以下的括號中。

Q 將部位名稱填入括號中。

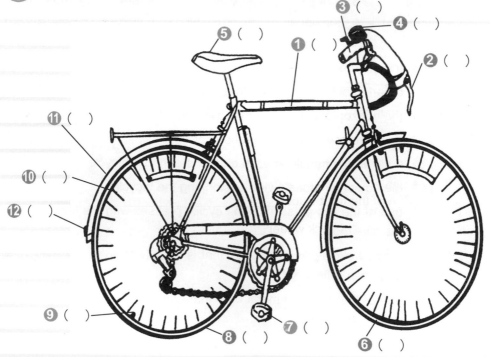

解題

① crossbar;　② brake;　③ handlebar;　④ bell;　⑤ seat;

⑥ rim;　⑦ pedal;　⑧ tyre;　⑨ valve;　⑩ spoke;　⑪ mudguard;　⑫ reflector

☺ 救回被遺忘的英文：**自行車可能會出現的狀況**

　　自行車總是難免會出狀況。可能會有哪些狀況呢？挑出適合的「狀況」說法，完成下面的句子。

Q 完成句子。

has broken	are rusty	Is clogged with dirt	often fail
has a puncture	often comes off	doesn't ring properly	is loose

① The chain of my bike ＿＿＿＿＿＿＿＿＿＿＿＿＿＿＿＿＿＿＿.

② The front tyre of his bike ＿＿＿＿＿＿＿＿＿＿＿＿＿＿＿＿＿＿.

③ My brakes ＿＿＿＿＿＿＿＿＿＿＿＿＿＿＿＿ on the slippery roads.

④ One of the pedals on her bike ＿＿＿＿＿＿＿＿＿＿＿＿＿＿＿＿.

⑤ The valve of the front wheel ＿＿＿＿＿＿＿＿＿＿＿＿＿＿＿＿.

⑥ The spokes of my back wheel ＿＿＿＿＿＿＿＿＿＿＿＿＿＿＿＿.

⑦ My bell ＿＿＿＿＿＿＿＿＿＿＿＿＿＿＿＿＿＿＿＿＿＿＿.

　　方框中，有些「狀況」的說法非常精確，講的是很特定的狀況。其他的說法則可以拿來描述自行車幾乎所有部位的問題。舉例來說，**has broken**就是一個非常好用的說法，可以拿來描述各個部位出現的問題。

再看一次方框裡的說法，判斷一下哪些用來描述特定的問題，哪些可以用來描述各式各樣的問題。在特定的問題說法旁邊寫下 S（Specific），在比較概括的問題說法旁邊寫下 G（General）。

想告訴別人自己的自行車有問題時，可以使用 "... need(s) + v.-ing" 的句型。想想看，有哪些動詞可以在這種情況派上用場呢？

Q 完成下面的句子。

8 My back tyre _____.

9 My brakes _____.

10 One of my spokes _____.

11 My valve _____.

12 The left pedal of my bicycle _____.

解題

自行車可能會有以下這些問題：

The chain of my bike often comes off（常常掉鏈子）. The front tyre of his bike has a puncture（前輪有洞）. My brakes often fail on the slippery roads（在濕滑的路上騎車時剎車很容易失靈）. One of the pedals on her bike has broken（有一個踏板壞了）. The valve of the front wheel is clogged with dirt（前輪氣嘴閥被泥塞住了）. The spokes of my back wheel are rusty（後輪輪輻生銹了）. My bell doesn't ring properly（車鈴不響故障了）.

doesn't ring properly，often fail on the slippery roads，has a puncture都是比較精確的說法，只能搭配the bell，the brakes，the tyre使用。其他的問題都是比較概括性的，可以搭配自行車的任何部位使用。

在描述自行車的問題時，可以使用repair，mend，replace等單字。因此，第8至12句也可以填入這些說法：need(s) mending，need(s) repairing，need(s) replacing。

 救回被遺忘的英文：試著閱讀關於自行車的文章

以下的兩篇文章都和自行車的主題相關。先快速閱讀一遍，並判斷這些文章是從哪裡來的（百科全書？雜誌？報紙？日記？信件？手冊？小說？）、寫作風格（正式還是不正式？）、大概的主題是什麼。

 閱讀下面兩篇文章，完成句子。

Text 3 is probably from a(n) _____.

The style is _____.

The general topic is _____.

Text 4 is probably from a(n) _____.

The style is _____.

The general topic is _____.

Text 3

Forty million bicycles were made last year, according to the China Bicycle Association. About 420 million Chinese ride bicycles, to keep fit as well as to get around. About 7 million ride bikes in Beijing, which has a total population of more than 10 million. China produced 10 million bicycles in 1979. The number rose to 20 million in 1982, and 40 million last year. China exports 10 million bicycles annually.

Text 4

Beijing is big but it's quite easy to get around. There are buses, taxis and an underground system but I go almost everywhere by bike! It's fantastic. Fortunately, bike-theft is not as big a problem here as it is at home. There are special bike lanes all over the city, so although the roads are busy, I feel quite safe. I can't believe how convenient it is. There are bike repairmen on almost every corner so I never need to worry about breaking down or getting a puncture. Cycling makes me feel so independent — just being able to go where I want, when I choose, is a luxury. Whenever I see people waiting at bus stops, I wonder why they don't just go by bike instead. The buses always look terribly crowded and uncomfortable. Some of the other foreign teachers here use taxis a lot but I actually think cycling is preferable because it's helping me get to know Beijing and making me feel "part of things". And, of course, it's the cheapest way to get around — apart from walking. Distances here are so great that it's usually not possible to go anywhere on foot. So, I'm having a great time and getting quite fit too.

解題

Text 3 is probably from a newspaper article (published possibly many years ago).

The style is formal.

The general topic is the increase in bicycle production and use (which can be called the "bike boom") in China.

Text 4 is probably from a personal letter.

The style is informal.

The general topic is cycling in Beijing (or the pleasures of cycling in Beijing).

救回被遺忘的英文：指出正確的資訊

閱讀並判斷下面的句子是否是在Text 3中出現的資訊。在其中出現的資訊前面打個勾（√）。已經為你完成了一個範例！

Q 在Text 3中提到的内容前面打勾（√）。

____√____ ⓐ the number of Chinese people who ride bicycle

_____ ⓑ the population of China

_____ ⓒ the number of bicycles produced in China this year

_____ ⓓ the number of bicycles produced in China each year

_____ ⓔ the number of bicycles produced in China in 1982

_____ ⓕ the rapid growing of bicycle production

_____ **g** the annual amount of bicycle exports in China

_____ **h** the advantages of cycling

_____ **i** the number of Beijing residents who ride bicycles

_____ **j** the population of Beijing

_____ **k** the bicycle lanes in Beijing

_____ **l** the problems brought by so many bicycles

_____ **m** bike-theft in Beijing

_____ **n** the new-generation bicycles

解題

在Text 3中提到的資訊是：**e**, **f**, **g**, **i**, **j**

😃 救回被遺忘的英文：**說出騎自行車的優點**

有些人騎自行車是因為他們只能靠這個方式出遊，還有些人則是自己選擇騎自行車的。Text 4是一名來到北京的外國專家寫的信。從信的內容來看，寫信者很享受騎車。這位寫信者提到了至少八種騎車的好處，是哪些好處呢？請寫在下面。

Q 閱讀Text 4，寫下其中提到的八種騎車的優點。

❶ _____

❷ _____

❸ _____

❹ _____

❺ _____

❻ _____

❼ _____

❽ _____

解題

寫信者提到的騎車的優點有：

❶ It is very convenient（很方便）.

❷ It is safe（很安全）.

❸ It makes the writer feel so independent（讓寫信者覺得自己很獨立）.

❹ It is not as crowded and uncomfortable as taking the buses（不像搭公車那樣又擠又不舒服）.

❺ It helps the writer get to know Beijing（讓寫信者更了解北京）.

❻ It makes the writer feel "part of things"（讓寫信者覺得自己能融入進來）.

❼ It is the cheapest way to get around — apart from walking（是除了步行外最便宜的交通方式）.

❽ By cycling, the writer is getting quite fit too（騎車讓寫信者身體健康）.

救回被遺忘的英文：如何在閱讀中找細節

再閱讀Text 4一遍，回答問題。

Q 閱讀並回答問題。

1 What other means of transport are there in Beijing, according to the writer?

_____

2 Why does the writer feel safe when riding a bicycle in Beijing?

_____

3 Is bike-theft a big problem in Beijing as it is in the writer's hometown?

_____

4 Why doesn't the writer worry about punctures and so on?

_____

5 Why doesn't the writer do much walking?

_____

6 What does the writer mean by saying that "cycling makes me feel so independent"?

_____

_____

7 What does the writer mean by saying that cycling is making her feel "part of things"?

_____

_____

解題

1 Buses, taxis and underground.

2 Because there are special bike lanes all over Beijing.

3 No.

4 Because there are bike repairmen on almost every corner.

5 Because she thinks distances are so great in Beijing.

6 She is able to go where she wants, when she chooses.

7 She is getting to know more about the city and getting used to its life style so she feels that she is really living there (and not just a visitor).

Part 6——
讓你的英文能力起死回生！
最常見的交通方式

 救回被遺忘的英文：討論各種交通方式的優點和缺點

在Part 5中，我們請你寫下在Text 4中寫信者提到的在北京騎自行車的所有優點。那麼，騎自行車有什麼缺點呢？其他的交通工具又有哪些優點及缺點呢？

我們先來討論最常見的四種交通工具：自行車（bike），公車（bus），地鐵（underground）及計程車（taxi）。你覺得使用這些交通工具有哪些優點呢？在思考「優點」的時候，可以看看下面方框裡面提到的正面形容詞（positive adjectives），在思考「缺點」的時候，可以試試用這些正面形容詞的反義詞或否定形式。當然，你可以用的不只以下這些形容詞，還可以想一些與眾不同的答案。

 寫下不同交通方式的優點。

| quick | cheap | convenient | healthy |
| safe | clean | comfortable | reliable |

Forms of transport	Advantages	Disadvantages
Travelling by bike		
Travelling by bus		
Travelling by underground		
Travelling by taxi		

Q 使用以下句型練習大聲說：

Travelling by _____ is _____. It is also _____.

And it is _____, too. (OR: But it's _____.)

🔔 解題

以下解答僅供參考用，因為大家對各種交通工具的優缺點看法不一樣！你也可能寫出完全不一樣的答案。

Travelling by bike is convenient, cheap, healthy ...; It is slower than other forms of transport. It is less comfortable in bad weather. It is rather tiring for long distances ...

Travelling by bus is convenient, cheap, safe ...; It is uncomfortable when there are many people in the bus. It is unreliable when there are traffic jams. It is dirty in bad weather ...

Travelling by underground is quick, safe, reliable ...; It is uncomfortable when there are too many people. It is inconvenient in certain places where there are few underground stations. It is not very healthy to take it all the time ...

Travelling by taxi is quick, comfortable, convenient, clean ...; But it is much more expensive, and it is not always possible to find a taxi when you need one ...

😀 救回被遺忘的英文：如何描述去上班或上學的路

Text 5是一封寫給大衛的信（你還記得大衛嗎？他是這個單元一開始提到的客座專家）。寫信的人是大衛在英國的朋友，他最近開始在一座新城市上大學。

閱讀這封信的一部分（有標號碼的地方），看看以下表格，把信中提到的資訊打勾（√），並寫下句子的號碼。

 把信中提到的資訊打勾（√），並寫下句子前的數字。

Letter extract	Details mentioned	Sentence No.
season of the year		
temperature of the day		
location of home		
time of departure from home		
things passed on the way		
activities on the way		
location of study place		
companion(s)		
usual way of travelling		
alternative way of travelling		
distance to/from bus stop		
comparative comment(s)		
(general) comment(s)		

續表

Letter extract	Details mentioned	Sentence No.
time of usual journey		
time of alternative journey		
cost of journey		
time of arrival at study place		
time spent in the university		
time of going back home		

Text 5

(1) Now I study at the university, which is in the town centre. (2) My home is on the outskirts of the town, about one and a half miles from the university. (3) There is a regular bus service between the two but I prefer to walk when the weather's fine. (4) It's a pleasant walk, downhill all the way! (5) It takes me about forty minutes and I spend the time enjoying the peace and quiet of the early morning and thinking about the day ahead. (6) I pass a lovely old church on the way and have to cross the river. (7) Sometimes, if I have time, I stop to chat to one or two people on the way. (8) If it's raining, I have to take the bus. (9) The bus journey itself is quick but it's a long walk from my house to the bus stop and then from the bus stop to the university. (10) So it's actually quicker to do the whole journey on foot! (11) It's cheaper too. (12) The bus costs 2 pounds, which is quite expensive for such a short distance ...

解題

信中所提到的資訊如下：

location of home (2); things passed on the way (6); activities on the way (5, 6, 7); location of study place (1); usual way of travelling (3); alternative way of travelling (8); distance to/from bus stop (9); comparative comment(s) (10, 11); (general) comment(s) (4); time of usual journey (5); cost of journey (12)

救回被遺忘的英文：如何觀察信中所使用的詞句

　　現在來看看信中用了哪些詞句吧！這封信並不正式，因為是寫給朋友的，但條理很清晰。

Q　觀察信中使用的詞句。

❶ What is the main tense of the text? Why does the writer use this tense?

_____

_____.

❷ The writer uses "if" to indicate possible alternatives. Find two examples from the text.

a. _____.

b. _____.

3 You may have noticed that the pronoun "it" is used several times in the text, but refers to different things. Find one example for the following.

a. "It" stands for the journey:

_____.

b. "It" stands for an action:

_____.

c. "It" stands for the weather:

_____.

 解題

1 The main tense used in the text is simple present tense, because the writer is describing something he does almost every day.

2 a. Sometimes, if I have time, I stop to chat to one or two people on the way.
b. If it's raining, I have to take the bus.

3 a. It's a pleasant walk, downhill all the way.
b. It takes me about forty minutes ...
c. If it's raining, I have to take the bus.

Part 7——
讓你的英文能力起死回生！
請試著寫出一篇作文

 學完這一單元，你就可以：

☐ 閱讀地點介紹或地圖，並從中獲取資訊

☐ 依據地圖的指示找路

☐ 問路或為人指路

☐ 描述地標

☐ 知道各種交通方式，或詢問交通方式的相關問題

☐ 了解自行車的各個部位**並**討論自行車的相關問題

☐ 描述各種不同的交通方式的優缺點

☐ 描述一段短程旅行

　　這個單元已經結束了！你現在應該已經能夠很有自信地幫外國人指路了吧！就算是在國外迷路的話也不害怕了！請再**復**習一遍整個單元，寫下你遇到的所有問題。

😊 救回被遺忘的英文：如何描述你去上班或上學的途中見聞

　　參考Part 6中的Text 5，使用類似的句子順序，在筆記本中寫下一段（約15—20句）短文，描述自己去上班或上學的途中見聞。這段描述中，也可以提到252頁—253頁的表格裡寫到的所有資訊。如果覺得你的文章讓你滿意，就抄到作業本上吧！

將你去上班或上學的途中見聞寫成一篇文章。

請給它命名這個標題：

My Routine Trip to Work (or School)

_____

_____

_____

_____

_____

_____

_____

_____

_____

_____

_____

_____

_____

_____

總復習

依照指示找到正確的路

　　喬治邀請海倫到他家吃晚餐，但海倫不知道他家怎麼走，於是喬治透過電話指示她怎麼走。

聽聽喬治的指示，為地圖上標數字的建築標出正確的名稱。

Track 017

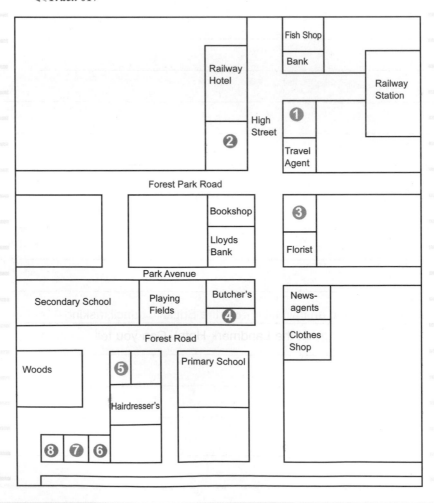

MP3音檔內容完整看

　　若是聽完音檔還是沒把握，建議可搭配本部份學習，不熟的語彙要查辭典並作筆記，方能加深英文記憶。

 Part 4: Track 016 　　（請配合230頁及音檔使用）

Jin Hong: Wei?

David: Hello, Jin Hong. This is David.

Jin Hong: Hi, David. Anything wrong?

David: No, no. Could you spare me a minute or two?

Jin Hong: You needn't be that polite. What can I do for you?

David: I've just had an invitation from the British Council, asking me to attend a welcome party at the Landmark Hotel. Can you tell me the best way to get to the hotel?

Jin Hong: Oh, it's quite a long way, but it's not difficult to get there. It's probably too far to go by bike ... so you'll have to take a bus.

David: I don't have a bike anyway.

Jin Hong: Then you take a bus. It's usually rather crowded.

David: That doesn't matter. Is there a direct bus to the hotel?

Jin Hong: Yes. You can take bus Te 8.

David: Where should I get off?

Jin Hong: At Liangmaqiao Station.

David: How often do the buses run?

Jin Hong: I'm not sure ... but probably about every 15 minutes.

David: How long does it take?

Jin Hong: Well, about one hour and 15 minutes. By the way, you could also go by taxi. That will be a bit more expensive but faster, and you always have a seat.

David: What is the fare if I take the bus?

Jin Hong: About two *yuan*.

David: And if I take a taxi?

Jin Hong: No more than fifty *yuan*.

David: I think I will take a taxi as it's more comfortable. Thanks for all your help.

Jin Hong: You're welcome. Feel free to call me again if you have more questions.

George: Okay, so you're arriving by train, right, Helen?

Helen: Yes, I think that's the most convenient, because I'll come straight from work.

George: Well, you come out of the Railway Station and turn left at the end of the road. Walk past the post office, which is on the corner, and past the travel agent, till you get to the crossroads.

Helen: Okay. Is the Railway Hotel anywhere near?

George: Yes, the Railway Hotel is directly in front of you as you walk up from the station. So, when you see it, turn left.

Helen: I remember there's a pub next to it. What's it called?

George: The Rose and Crown. But that will be on the other side of the road from you.

Helen: All right. I know where I am now. So, what do I do at the crossroads?

George: You cross diagonally, so go straight towards the bookshop.

Helen: Oh, yes. I remember the bookshop. It's opposite The Tea Rooms, isn't it?

George: Yes, that's right. The Tea Rooms are on the railway side, next to a florist. Anyway, go past the bookshop down High Street and take the second turning right after that. There's a bank on the corner.

Helen: It's Lloyds Bank, isn't it?

George: No, that's the road before, Park Avenue. You don't want that one. You want the next one. It's Forest Road. The bank ... it's the Royal Bank, I think ... it's next to a butcher's shop. Anyway, turn right into Forest Road after the bank. Okay?

Helen: Right. I've got that.

George: Now, you'll see a primary school on your left and playing fields on your right. Go straight on till you see the second turning on the left. It's opposite the secondary school.

Helen: Opposite the school ... okay. That's your road, isn't it?

George: Yes, it's Forest Crescent. There's a little grocer's on the corner and some woods opposite. Go past the grocer's, then past the hairdresser's ... It's quite a big salon.

Helen: Ah-ha, past the hairdresser's.

George: Now, you'll see the road bends right there and there are three houses on the left. The first house you come to belongs to that doctor you met with me once at a concert. Do you remember, Dr. Smith?

Helen: Oh, yes, the one with the lovely Thai wife.

George: Yes, that's right. Well, that's their house, number 3. Mine is the middle one, number 5. There's a big tree outside. Oh, and by the way ... guess who lives on the other side at number 7?

Helen: Who?

George: The guy you once went out with, Tom Black.

Helen: Oh, no. I hope he's not coming to dinner, is he?

George: No, don't worry. He's away on holiday at the moment.

Helen: So, what time do you want me there?

George: Well, if you get the 6:30 train, it'll get you to the station here at 7:15, and it'll take you about 15 minutes to walk from the station, so let's say 7:30?

Helen: Right, 7:30 sounds fine. See you tomorrow then.

George: Bye, see you.

語研力 **E064**

回溯式學習英語會話：
先聽說再讀寫，大量測驗的刻意練習，提升英語各項能力

不必從頭來，省一半的學習力氣，輕鬆說一口流利英語，聽說讀寫齊頭並進。

作　　者	顧曰國◎主編
顧　　問	曾文旭
出版總監	陳逸祺、耿文國
主　　編	陳蕙芳
執行編輯	翁芯俐
內文排版	李依靜
封面設計	李依靜
法律顧問	北辰著作權事務所

印　　製	世和印製企業有限公司
初　　版	2022 年 04 月

（本書改自《10年英語不白學，日常英語無師自通（附贈▋外師親錄強效學習MP3，日常英語聽力口說同步訓練！）》）

出　　版	凱信企業集團 - 凱信企業管理顧問有限公司
電　　話	（02）2773-6566
傳　　真	（02）2778-1033
地　　址	106 台北市大安區忠孝東路四段 218 之 4 號 12 樓
信　　箱	kaihsinbooks@gmail.com

定　　價	新台幣 349 元 / 港幣 116 元
產品內容	1 書

總 經 銷	采舍國際有限公司
地　　址	235 新北市中和區中山路二段 366 巷 10 號 3 樓
電　　話	（02）8245-8786
傳　　真	（02）8245-8718

國家圖書館出版品預行編目資料

回溯式學習英語會話－先聽說再讀寫，大量測驗的
刻意練習，提升英語各項能力／顧曰國著. – 初版.
– 臺北市：凱信企業集團凱信企業管理顧問有限公
司, 2022.04
　面；　公分
ISBN 978-626-7097-12-0(平裝)

1.CST: 英語 2.CST: 會話
805.188　　　　　　　　　　　111003842